About the author

C. M. Morrison works, when forced, as a surveyor. After twenty-five years in Yorkshire he has now retreated to Northumberland where he lives with his wife, dogs, and would be vegetable patch. Ultimately, he plans to return to Scotland in the next decade or so.

FANG

Dedication

To everyone who has made
me laugh over the years

C. M. Morrison

FANG

REDARROW
BOOKS

A CIP catalogue record for this title is
available from the British Library.

ISBN 978 1 84433 009 6

*RedArrow Books is an imprint of
Austin & Macauley Publishers Ltd.*

First Published in 2011

RedArrow Books
CGC-33-01, 25 Canada Square
Canary Wharf, London E14 5LQ

The paper used in this product is grown in sustainable forests

Printed & Bound in Great Britain

Prologue

Bleakhope Tower lurked in a dourly furtive fashion amongst the trees and shrubs that had sprung up around it since its heyday. To anyone who felt the need to examine its ancient charms, it presented an implacably hostile face remarkably similar to the expression habitually worn by its former owners. Overtaken by events in the form of the unification of Scotland and England and the advent of gunpowder, it stood empty and forgotten, only its name living on as the title of the tattered remnants that was the remaining estate of the Fangs following Royal displeasure, the joy of gambling, Liberal taxation and an inability to prosper at anything since reiving and feuding went out of fashion.

Strangely, it had never suffered the indignity of being used as a source of building material for farms and houses, possibly its air of malevolence helped ensure it remained untouched; perhaps it was merely the effort that demolition would have entailed. Whatever the reason, it waited with feral cunning and vicious expectation through the centuries for the old days to return. Due to a sudden burst of passion and sexual activity it was not disappointed...

Chapter 1

John Fang farmed the remaining Bleakhope Estates when he could be bothered, pottered amongst the records of his family for pleasure and, when forced to remember, acted out the part of the local Laird at sporadic intervals. An inveterate correspondent, he was a joy to history students throughout the world who were studying either the Marches Legellum of the old Anglo Scots border or the involvement of his forebears in shady, invariably bloody, little known historical events. He could quote verbatim the speech of the then Laird just before the Battle of Flodden. Paraphrased, it amounted to "Everyman for himsel" and Deil take the hindmost". Due to retaining their full complement of manpower unlike their more loyal fellow subjects, the Fangs had risen high in the years that followed. Unsurprisingly, the family motto had become "For Himsel". John Fang had followed this creed unerringly, paying scant regard for anyone other than himself and none at all to the difficulties that would face his heir.

Unlike his ancestors, Fang was not a bad or vicious man. The thought of him lifting cattle or hacking his way to the top was impossible to contemplate. He had, however, a full quota of the renowned Fang stubbornness. Once he gripped an idea he hung onto the bitter end. This was what finally killed him.

Sonya Birtle had grown bored with life in London. From an early age she had been both promiscuous and inventive. Sadly, the males of her acquaintance had lacked the latter attribute and were politically incorrect in their views on sex. She had become bored with satisfying everyone but herself. Although it surprised those who thought that they knew her, it was typical that she would be seized with a passionate interest in Fang when she read an article written by him in a magazine she had picked up at the dentist. Acting on the spur of the moment, she set off North in her car having telephoned the office to say that she was ill. Unknown to her, this was assumed to mean pregnant but the fact was never mentioned on her return, her fellow workers merely thinking the worst.

At first she had been disappointed in Fang. He was too otherworldly in his attitudes and he lacked the naked ambition of nearly every other man she had met. He improved, however, as soon as she got him talking about his family history and had worked himself into a fine passion reciting little known facts and legends. Unknown to Sonya, Fang had also developed a strong interest in her body if not her mind. The only way which he found he could hold her attention was by telling the old tales with panache and a strong tendency towards Scott at his most flowery. This served its purpose in so far as she paid him close attention rather than assuming her normal, vacant, expression.

They sat late over a guttering fire of poorly stacked, damp wood that Sonya felt was atmospheric and Fang felt was typical. They had made inroads into his paltry collection of wine and he was trying to calculate if he dared ask her to stay the night. She, in turn, was making every possible hint that it would be worth his time to ask her to stay as she was only too well aware of the state of her bank balance and she had not seen anything resembling a hotel in the area. After stretching in a manner that showed her to maximum advantage several times and caused Fang to slurp his wine too quickly, she gazed soulfully at him.

"Do you mind awfully if I sleep here tonight? I mean..." Fang totally misunderstood her.

"Of course, yes, indeed, after all that wine, yes, much better..." His apparent disinterest worked on her like an aphrodisiac to her total surprise. Was this what she had been missing all the time in London, the challenge of a man who failed to become aroused when she looked? Whatever the reason she was in little doubt of the effect on her body. Fang sat unmoving, terrified that she would see the total arousal her innocent stretching had caused. Unknowingly, he served his cause well by waving a hand towards the stairs.

"Find a bed up there." He paused and gulped some more wine. "What time breakfast? Show you the estate tomorrow."

Sonya slept well having rapidly climaxed as her fingers pretended to be Fang. He did not.

The next morning, she woke well rested and immediately thought of her new challenge and flushed with excitement. She dressed with care. Fang had risen early and drowned his inner

15

devils to no avail in a cold bath. She found him morosely hunched over a mug of coffee in the dilapidated kitchen next to the unlit Aga. He looked terribly romantic, she thought, dark mooded with a sense of brooding danger. Fang felt exhausted. She smiled brightly at him and he recovered sufficiently to find her a mug of coffee. She wandered around the room and stood at the window where the morning light streamed into the room. It also served to turn her dress translucent as he had hoped, and Fang revived to a state of mug chewing lust. She turned and faced him, holding her mug in both hands so that she could peep seductively at him as she sipped. "I'm sure you're terribly busy so when would it be convenient to look over the estate? I mean, I can wander about myself if that's all right..."

Fang spilled his coffee as he started as her announcement interrupted his lecherous thoughts. "No. No. Promised, after breakfast, yes." He started to mop at himself and then stopped, sure he would look as silly as he felt, a middle-aged man ineffectually pawing himself as she watched. Sonya gazed at him raptly. She could be happy here, she thought. Turned on by his indifference, surrounded by history and magazine induced romantic visions. The thing was to make him see things the same way. And that old-fashioned, clipped speech, she shivered with excitement.

After an unappetising breakfast of well-fired bacon and underdone toast, Sonya set about capturing the Laird of Bleakhope. She gushed happily at varnish smothered pictures of ancestors indistinguishable from their dogs except for the friendlier expressions on the animals dimly seen faces. She gazed raptly through the dusty windows of the drawing room at the early spring sunlight that reflected off the river running below them, and exclaimed at the stark outline of Bleakhope tower, which she spotted squatting disconsolately among the trees. John Fang gradually came awake. His simple tactics of keeping her between him and the windows served to provide him with exciting silhouettes. Allied to her obvious interest in all things ancient, this visual stimulation helped him gain confidence and he showed his wide knowledge of useless if intriguing facts. Sonya heard the tale behind the family's second motto "Bite ane, bitten by a", and was treated to a personal rendition of the ballad "The Bleakhope

Feast", which celebrated the boiling of a rival to the wardenship of the old Scots West March.

Aware that she had him thoroughly interested at last and that if she played her cards right she could become lady of all she surveyed, Sonya asked brightly if the view was better upstairs. The snort of assent from Fang signalled the end of his indifference to her charms and she skipped excitedly ahead of him up the stairs. Innocently wide-eyed she stopped at what she presumed was the entrance to his bedroom. "Here?" she enquired brightly.

"Linen cupboard, no view," he replied and opened a much smaller door to the right. His spaniel, a decrepit and flatulent beast, followed them in unseen. It lacked loyalty but not curiosity.

The views were not startling, but Sonya stopped and turned so sharply before she reached the window that Fang walked into her. She giggled and threw her arms around his neck. "You are masterful," she giggled in a little come to bed voice.

Ignoring the sane inner voice that muttered darkly about his age and unfitness, Fang swept her off the floor and carried her to the bed where he dropped her as his arms gave out. She gasped with delight at this rough, dominant behaviour and sat up to wriggle out of her dress and panties in an instant. Fang stared in stunned delight at her. She gave a little shiver of lust that jiggled her breasts and he was totally lost. Sonya sprawled back on the bed in open invitation and he tore off his clothes in a frenzy. Climbing onto the bed beside her he gazed raptly into her eyes and, as he prepared to touch her with a quivering hand, the spaniel broke wind noisily and horribly. "Bloody animal!" He scrambled off the bed and chased it out the door before turning in a sweat of lust for the bed and its occupant once more.

"Hurry, I can't wait," she encouraged him and he followed orders. Sonya screamed in ecstasy then again in horror as he entered her and died.

She shoved him off with difficult and sat up. "Oh bugger," she said tearfully. She pulled on her dress and panties again and sat on the edge of the bed considering. She could tell he was dead. The unhealthy flush on his face, she did not want to look elsewhere now, and the sudden lack of breath did not require a medical degree to interpret. She couldn't leave him like this she decided. The questions would be too embarrassing and she had no wish to

17

become involved. It took her several minutes to partially dress him again without looking, and she was exhausted when she finished. She went downstairs and found the telephone.

The local GP arrived ahead of the ambulance. He looked at the remains of Fang who appeared to be smiling for the first time that he could remember and at Sonya who, despite her obvious shock still managed to look sexy. He took in the fact that she was wearing a light summer dress, no bra and no shoes despite the coldness of the day.

"Aye" he pondered. " Not a bad way to go lass, don't you agree?" She sniffed and looked at him. He winked and looked at the body again. "Nothing for either of us here now I'd say. We'll leave it to the ambulance crew to sort things with Mrs Burns down the village. She threatened to keep the place tidy I believe." He held open the door. "You'll be away again I imagine?" Sonya agreed that she would. "Well, nothing to worry anyone about here, his heart just gave out. Heard the bang did you?" She giggled despite herself. "Just as I thought. Well, well."

It was only when she was heading back South that Sonya realised that she had no idea who would take over from Fang. It might be worth coming back one day even if only to revisit the scene of the best screw that had never happened. She wept over a coffee at Moffat. "Fang, you bastard," she muttered to herself. She was not the first and certainly would not be the last to curse that name.

Chapter 2

The rattle of mail through the letterbox did not cheer Ian Hallshaw in any way. Rather, he slumped lower into his chair and bowed his head so that he nearly drowned in the oversized coffee mug that he clutched two handed. He glanced over towards the bed that filled nearly half of his bedsit and viewed its occupant dispassionately. From what he remembered of the previous night, the red head was inventive but no conversationalist. He sighed and rose, wincing, to review the latest bundle of bills and final demands that the postman had delivered. Returning to his chair, he sorted morosely through the post, tearing open envelopes and dividing them into circulars, bills and lawyer headed missives that he left in three piles unread on the table. Sighing deeply, he blundered back to bed pushing the girl over to make room. For a short while he gazed at the ceiling before exhaustion overcame both anxiety and hangover and he fell asleep. He woke with a start to find his companion suddenly talkative if repetitive.

"Well, are you going to?" she kept repeating in excited tones.

His response was masterly. "What the hell are you on about?" This was the first intimation he received that the hard gripping curse of the Fangs was about to enter his life although he did not recognise the danger. She knelt astride him and waved the letter in an excited fashion that drew his eyes irresistibly to her breasts.

"Are you going to?" she demanded again, only to realise that Hallshaw had misunderstood her question and, revitalised after his sleep, was carrying on where he had left off the previous night.

Later, as she lay across his chest and he waited for his breathing to quieten, he noticed she was clutching a crumpled letter in her fist. "What's with the letter?"

"That's what I was asking," she twitched the letter vaguely in his direction. "Are you going to?" Hallshaw decided the simplest way to gain information was to imitate her brevity.

"What?" he enquired, twitching his head in the vague direction of the missive.

"Change your name so you can inherit?" Words failed him and he rolled over on top and, seizing the letter, rested it on her breasts to read it. The girl threw a vaguely affectionate arm around him and seemed happy to wait for a reply as he rapidly scanned the letter then read it more slowly. She watched with interest as a grin spread slowly across his face.

"I take it that means yes," she murmured. By way of answer he hugged her fiercely and bounced, suddenly revitalised, out of bed and started rooting in the heap of clothes that lay on the floor.

"Ah!" He triumphantly stood up waving her mobile phone. "May I?"

"Yeah, if the battery has any power left."

Hallshaw dialled the number as shown on the letter and asked to be put through to Mr McFoul the letter's signator. To the girl on the bed's surprise, his voice had changed becoming more clipped and arrogant. "Hallshaw here, you wrote to me concerning an inheritance...Yes, that is correct...can you elaborate?" She listened with rapidly increasing interest while her mind grasped the concept of an inheritance. She was just considering how to keep Hallshaw interested when he flung the mobile phone to the floor in disgust. "The battery has died," he announced unsurprisingly.

She fished in her handbag and proffered him some change. "Call from downstairs and make an appointment to see him. You don't hear the pips these days." Hallshaw clutched the money and headed for the door. "Aren't you going to dress first?"

"It seems I now own a castle, estate and various parts of Scotland!" he announced on his return. She smiled sweetly and stretched to advantage.

"Come and tell me all about it." He hopped onto the bed and chattered happily, while she used her undeniable talents to advantage until he lost interest even in his new estate for the pleasure of the moment. She had no intention of missing a chance to land one of the gentry. "What name do you have to take?" she enquired in a muffled voice.

"Fang," he replied, then screamed as she bit him in surprise.

The girl sat by the table watching Hallshaw as he sat dabbing carefully at his groin with a pack of frozen peas and a look of impotent fury on his face. She hoped that neither emotion nor action would last too long. It had seemed a sensible move to hop out of bed at the time, dressing quickly so that she could make a swift escape while he rolled around clutching himself in agony. When she had seen no sign that he was about to attack her, she had been sufficiently emboldened to find the frozen peas and pass them to him silently. Now, she tried to think of a way to ensure that he would not literally throw her out as soon as he felt physically able.

"What were you ancestors famous for?" she enquired, mock bright as a teacher.

"Killing people!" he snarled back through clenched teeth.

Looking at him, she found the idea all too believable. Hallshaw really did not know, but his small knowledge of the Borders made it seem likely and he felt like saying it. Unnoticed, the spirit of the Fangs had slipped into the room and had stated its dread work. Even when Hallshaw felt sufficiently recovered to stand up, he hobbled in a spavined fashion around the small room the girl watching sadly. Her plans, like his pride, in tatters. With an obvious effort, Hallshaw forced himself to consider his next move. The one, overriding factor sufficient for him to almost ignore the agony was the fact that he was now wealthy and the debts that had swamped him since he had left university could be wiped out.

Later that morning, Hallshaw walked with a strangely hesitant gait into the reception of McFoul and Company, Solicitors. Having been asked to take a seat and wait, the receptionist was surprised to notice him surreptitiously plucking at his groin and hissing discordantly through his clenched teeth. She found the sight so surprising that she answered the next incoming call with "Groin's can I help you?" McFoul, who had just stuck his head out of his office, raised an implacable if bushy eyebrow and invited Hallshaw in. Hallshaw hobbled past a disconcerted receptionist as she tried to convince an archdeacon that he must have misheard her.

McFoul waved a diffident hand. "Sit down, sit down." He observed Hallshaw's hesitant movements with interest. As his new client sat hissing in his now customary manner while holding himself gingerly, McFoul remembered the Venereal Disease lectures he had been forced to attend during National Service. "Spot of trouble?" he enquired. Hallshaw glared and McFoul

21

dropped the topic, mentally praising himself for his perception. "Yes. Well. The inheritance. Quite."

Silence hovered in the room as Hallshaw, remembering the speech patterns of certain older schoolmasters, waited. McFoul lifted a few papers from the various mounds that lay like yellowing snowdrifts across his desk. "Now, where was I?" He paused and then beamed with the triumph of a man who has defeated the system and waved a file in Hallshaw's direction. "Yes, the Fang inheritance. Quite." He looked at the file with interest then up at Hallshaw. "Did you know your uncle well?"

"Met him once when I was small. Good fun when you were seven, I've never seen him since. My mother has never mentioned her family. Strange but there it is." McFoul, with the knowledge gleaned from trying to look after the Fangs for many years felt that this showed common sense on the part of Hallshaw's mother, chose merely to nod.

"Well, as to what the inheritance means...oh, you do have proof of identity I suppose." Hallshaw proffered his birth certificate and passport, grimacing as he leant forward to do so.

McFoul took the documents. "Thank you, I can see the resemblance now." He observed as Hallshaw sat back scowling and hissing with pain. Indeed, he felt that Hallshaw bore a remarkable resemblance to his uncle when he contorted his face like that. Perhaps the gene pool was narrower than he had surmised.

"Yes, the inheritance. Your uncle was very proud of the name, not a problem to you, is it? I mean, you're not a dentist or anything like that?"

"No, right, the inheritance." Hallshaw impressed him with his very stillness; most men would have been leaning forward with eagerness to discover what fortune had in store for them, but not his new client. Hallshaw waited trying to ignore the fact that the effect of the frozen peas was fast wearing off as McFoul continued.

"In effect, you change your name to Fang and gain the estate. Bit of fishing and shooting, and whatever death duties do not remove. Farms are all let except Home Mains, bit of income but not much. Few cottages and so on. Got plenty money have you? Be rather a pleasant place when you do it up. One other thing, you must spend the majority of your time there. That's it in a nutshell."

Chapter 3

It was strange that the most modern of industries should have given rise to such an old-fashioned rivalry. In the manner of Italian Merchant Princes, the principles of Coretec and Fireflow IT loathed one another with a mutual passion. If either John Galphay or Brian Mickley had ever considered the fact that that their hatred for one another had driven both to success in a field where so many had failed, they would have dismissed the thought out of hand. Their individual success they attributed to personal ability, the others', to incomprehensible luck. Determined to out do one another they treated the Atlantic as an inconvenient ditch and the United States as an untapped market for their products. This very insouciance had appealed to the American public and led to their mutual growth in the face of all extraneous competition.

Strangely, both had become the opposite of how they had been before entering business. Mickley, the son of a bricklayer worked from an unreconstructed Victorian office block with tiled corridors that resembled an upmarket public convenience and that contained offices that were panelled in dark oak. He dressed and sounded like an Edwardian country solicitor, well-modulated tones wrapped in comfortable tweeds.

Galphay, coldly angered both by his parents' attempts to educate him privately and a pleasant middle-class upbringing as the son of an architect, spoke with an aggressive Yorkshire accent of indeterminate source and dressed as he wished, which was normally inappropriately. If Fireflow occupied a memorial to trade with an empire on which the sun never set, Coretec worked in an office of such modernity and with a lighting system of such intensity that no one could have slept even if they had dared to try.

A rapidly concocted piece for the Business Section of a Quality Sunday by a harassed Sub Editor with half a page to fill when an inconvenient journalist failed to file his copy due to his predilection for cocaine, a habit that was soon to become too expensive to maintain as one of the unemployed whom he had previously decried, caused the first tremor that was to lead to the rejuvenation of Bleakhope Tower and all it stood for.

On that fateful Monday morning, Mickley was working through the correspondence file his PA had left on his desk. When she returned with his coffee, he cleared his throat in a self-depreciating fashion. "Sheila, I cannot help feeling our people are to similar to the, um, opposition. They have the same qualifications, attend the same courses. Result? Similar approach, similar outcome, mm?"

Sheila, being a perceptive girl, could see where this was heading, she had also read the article. Accordingly, she covered herself by checking her personnel files on junior staff were up to date in anticipation of her employer's request when she returned to collect the correspondence file and his empty cup. She stood and waited while he verbally pottered with several mmm's mentally weighing his words before making his pronouncement.

Finally he spoke. "We need a new way of team building, strengthen links and empower creativity, mm?" Sheila gazed silently back remembering how long the last member of staff who had tried something different had survived. No one of any seniority or time within the company would suggest or consider anything out of the ordinary if not directed to do so by Mickley himself. And what did he mean by empower creativity? Mickley gazed back at her. "Need a new approach to training," he finally announced.

Sheila proffered her file. "Our people who are best suited to identifying a new approach." Mickley raised his eyebrows. "They have been here the least time, well qualified and keen to make their mark and not unduly influenced by what has gone before."

"Ah." Mickley took the file and scanned the profiles swiftly. "Ask Miss Sweetness to come up please."

"Certainly, I believe you will find it is Ms Sweetness," she responded and left the room.

Across town, Galphay was providing the caring and considerate leadership for which he was renowned. "What the hell do you useless sods mean you don't know?" He glared at his assembled senior staff who shuffled and found the view across the open plan office, where their staff had adopted the Coretec position, head down and ears open to pick up the latest management trend to adopt, vaguely dispiriting. "By, you'd be useless without me. It's obvious our training lacks something. Bunch of sheep you lot, we need something new, something to give us the edge. A paradigm." He stood hands on hips and glared around him. "Go on then, get managing and I want suggestions by coffee time." Stifling groans and plastering brightly innovative looks on their faces, they scurried back to their sections.

Whilst the majority of staff at Coretec considered the corporate hell that was their communal coffee break where Galphay held forth at length while ulcers blossomed and reputations and egos were shredded in the name of team building and openness, one member of staff sensed the opportunity he had been seeking. John Wear had recently joined Coretec and was still sufficiently callow to perceive the company as dynamic and innovative and providing opportunities for advancement singularly lacking in other more old-fashioned organisations. While waiting for coffee time he honed his thoughts and approach to getting noticed.

Alison Sweetness was petite, blonde and ruthlessly ambitious. Having spent six weeks at Fireflow losing potential friends and alienating people with remarkable speed and efficiency, her star was in the ascendant. Her constant, impeccably ill-timed questioning allied to her ability to produce efficient and worthwhile results meant she was loathed with increasing caution by her colleagues. It was obvious that she despised all around her and thought only of herself. It was equally apparent that she felt the only way was up and that her workmates represented only stepping stones for her progress. With the colossal self-confidence that was both her strength and weakness, she could only see positives in the summons to Mickley's office. Stopping only long enough in the ladies to remove her bra and undo one button too many in her blouse, she trotted upstairs to the Directors floor.

To the usual ten o'clock sighs, Coretec staff migrated towards the staff lounge area with the apathy of migrating wildebeest knowing that the local pride of lions is feeling peckish. The more perceptive knew that the moment the supposedly democratic gathering failed to garner positive mention in the press or Galphay grew bored it would cease. Only two men picked up their coffee mugs with anything approaching pleasure, Galphay because he knew he had the buggers rattled so that he would remain unchallenged, Wear because what he thought of as "The Main Chance" had arrived.

Mickley was courtesy personified when Alison Sweetness knocked quietly on his office door. "Do come in my dear, delighted you could find the time." His PA ensured the connecting door between their offices was left slightly ajar and sat down at her word processor and tried to calculate how long Ms Sweetness would have survived if she had not found the time to visit. "Have a seat. Bit of a problem, more of a challenge hmm?" Alison Sweetness gazed raptly back at him while trying to work out what Mickley was on about. She was unaware of any problem with her work and she doubted if her colleagues had dared to complain. "Training issues," Mickley continued. "Want you to take the lead, come up with something new, drive us forward, together but ruthless, know what I mean?" Alison Sweetness smiled brilliantly and sat slightly forward in her chair to ensure that her employer gained the benefit of his slightly higher chair. The application of reverse psychology pleased her.

"How thrilling," she responded. "When do I start?" Mickley's gaze moved up reluctantly to her face.

"Eh, oh, immediately."

"How long have I got and what grade will I have?" She smiled beautifully.

"Month to set it up, er..." She leant further forward in anticipation. "Five thousand increase and, um, extras." He waved a languid hand in illustration.

"So, a new contract then," she demanded unhesitatingly. Mickley regarded her with interest. If she was as efficient in her work as in maximising her opportunity here then she would bear watching.

"Of course my dear. My PA will organise it all. Better have your own office. Feel free to come to me at any time." Alison Sweetness, normally a ferocious feminist, happily ignored the avuncular my dear and rose swiftly.

"I look forward to doing so. Thank you."

Five minutes later she was wondering what pictures to put on her new office walls while her predecessor was escorted protesting from the premises. "But what have I done?"

"Nothing," was the blunt reply as he found himself on the pavement. "That was the problem."

Wear waited long enough for Galphay to get into his stride, demanding answers from his senior people to a concept that they had only had sufficient time to start to absorb, before making his contribution to telling effect. "If I may," he began brazenly.

"Feel bloody free," responded Galphay, a sentiment shared by those in the firing line and keen to escape.

"I cannot help believing that we merely need to readjust our focus on training, shift our approach so to speak through process re-engineering and mind mapping based on research and clarity." The gathering gazed at him with a mix of pity and misapprehension.

"What the hell is he on about?" A senior sales manager enquired of his deputy. The deputy smiled brightly.

"Haven't got a clue, but he'll keep the old man occupied."

"What the bloody hell do you mean?" enquired Galphay in tones not conducive to further explanation. Wear, partly out of desperation and partly because he did not wish to lose his chance, expounded furiously.

"We need to remove training from the office environment, allow thought and team building to flourish unhindered by daily routine. Establish better communication and a dynamic approach."

Galphay thought for a second. "Sounds promising. How?"

Wear amazed himself and his colleagues. "Give me a bloody chance and I'll tell you!"

Galphay laughed. "Right, you've ten days to pull something together and present it. You'll either get the boot or a promotion. Ok?"

Wear sensed those around him moving away from him. "Thank you," he answered brightly.

"Right, back to work you lot, time's money." The meeting broke up leaving Wear standing alone and sweatily loitering. What the hell was he going to do now? Suddenly resolute, he followed Galphay.

"I'll need time to do research," he began.

"Aye, and a vehicle no doubt. See my secretary and claim a better desk near me."

Chapter 4

Ian Fang sat slumped at the kitchen table in Bleakhope House feeling that little had changed other than his name in the weeks since he had succeeded his uncle as Laird of Bleakhope. He and Alice had left London rejoicing in the thought of their troubles being over. It had only taken a day on the estate to realise the truth in old McFoul comment regarding hoping he had plenty of money. The place had been cash starved for so long that anything of value had been long sold including any paintings of ancestral Fangs who were not readily identifiable as imbeciles. The estate farms were on long lets that fairly, or unfairly in Fang's opinion, reflected their value. The house itself was damp, old-fashioned and draughty. The elderly kitchen range puffed smoke in time to the wind that battered at the exterior of the property and Fang clutched his mug disconsolately. It was not what he had envisaged based on childish memories and ill-founded hope. On the way north, Alice and he had chatted brightly about the future and the pleasure they would have in turning around the estate following his uncle's negative stewardship. Now, he could only sympathise with the poor devil and fully understood his attempts to escape from reality through his books and his history. He watched the smoke issue from the range with a fatalistic look in his eyes. He sighed as Alice threw open the door increasing the already powerful draft that was playing on his neck. Unlike him, she did not seem willing to merely sit and suffer, perpetually seeking ways in which to alter the situation. From what he could see of her, muffled as she was under several layers of clothes for warmth, she had yet another idea to suggest on how to improve their circumstances. Fang was beginning to feel she would stop at nothing to ensure that she became chatelaine of a worthwhile estate.

Alice plumped her cocooned body on Fang's lap. "I've been thinking," she announced. Fang stifled a groan of dismay and physical discomfort, choosing merely to shift his position slightly. At least she was warm.

"Yes," he responded with a signal lack of enthusiasm.

"Why don't we advertise bed and breakfast here? Think of the ambience. And the vacant cottages, we could rent them to holiday makers."

"Money," he responded almost in reflex.

"Well, we wouldn't need to spend much, bit of paint for the cottages and furniture from the old stables, you know the stuff. I'm sure I could knock up curtains from something. Anyway, we could be economic with the truth and the Tourist Board won't pay a lot of attention if we sound grand enough."

Fang thought for about three seconds. "All right, we'll give it a shot but don't be too disappointed if no one comes, I mean, would you?"

"Well, no, but I know the place and we only need them here for one night for B and B. Anyway, people like cottages with character."

"Bloody awful character if you ask me, but we'll give it a go."

The next day Fang found himself morosely painting the roughcast inner walls of one of the former estate workers cottages. It did not seem to cover the plaster very efficiently; in fact the effect seemed to resemble a lizard's skin that was suffering from an unpleasant affliction akin to leprosy. The glass in the window frames rattled almost incessantly and he wondered if there was any putty amongst the bric a brac and general guddle in the old stables by the house. He had no intention of climbing onto the roof in this wind to check the slates but judging by the general smell of damp he reckoned half of them must have been missing. Still, if it did not rain while any one foolish enough came to stay they should get away with it. Once he had finished throwing paint on the walls he would take a strimmer to the environs of the cottage and try to make the waste ground look like grass although he did not hold out a lot of hope.

Undeterred by Fang's pessimism, Alice pressed on with trying to attract unwitting guests to Bleakhope. The local Tourist Board was suitably impressed by the address when she telephoned not to enquire too closely as to the facilities on offer. By using her credit card, despite its parlous state, she placed an advertisement in the

Evening Standard offering Bed and Breakfast accommodation and holiday cottages to let. This was ultimately to prove a fatal move but at the time seemed a golden opportunity to generate some income from the estate. While waiting to see if anyone was foolish enough to respond to the advertisements, Alice concentrated on hauling out ancient furniture and cleaning and repairing it sufficiently to place in the cottages. Despite her best efforts, the additions did little to enhance the cottages looking merely what they were, a haphazard accumulation that at best dwarfed their surroundings and, in some cases, served to make the state of the cottages look even worse than they were. Fang merely smiled sardonically when she asked his opinion and whistled a mournful little air he had learnt.

When the telephone rang, both Alice and Fang gazed at one another in surprise. "You never know, it might be some poor fool," Fang announced. "Better answer it."

"What do I say?" Alice regarded the instrument with sudden concern. In her heart she could not but help feel they were intending to take money under false pretences.

"Whatever you like, but hurry up."

"Bleakhope Hall, yes that is correct. Yes, I believe we may have a cottage available next week, allow me to check." She covered the mouthpiece and gazed at Fang who gaped back. "How much do I charge?"

"Christ!" Fang shook his head. "Try two fifty but don't push it."

"Hullo, yes, you're in luck. The cost? Two hundred and fifty pounds. In advance please." Suddenly overtaken by a sense of foreboding, she added, "It's quite basic but peaceful. I suppose you could call it atmospheric. Look forward to seeing you then. Bye."

Five days later, Tom MacDowell and his family gazed in horror at the living room of the cottage. "Well, they said it was atmospheric," He announced in the hope of cheering his wife. The attempt was unsuccessful, Tanya MacDowell had no intention of being cheered. She had hoped to go to Lanzarote and had foolishly let her husband persuade her that there would be plenty of last minute deals that would save them a small fortune. Due to the weather this had not been the case and she suspected him of planning a holiday in Scotland all along while merely humouring her with his talk of last minute bargains. The MacDowell children were equally unimpressed. They were too well aware of their father's predilection for holidays in Scotland to believe that he had ever intended anything other than a week in this hellhole. They knew only too well the mocking that would await them when they returned to school and confessed to another holiday spent fighting midges and walking in the rain.

Tanya MacDowell slumped dispiritedly into the settee that appeared to be suffering from a painful hernia and half vanished from sight. "For God's sake get me out," she wailed. Her husband chose to believe that she merely meant from the clammy grip of the furniture.

"Let's have a look around", he suggested once he had helped his wife regain her feet. Led by the children and assisting his limping wife, MacDowell headed for the stairs. He had just planted his foot on the first tread when his children started screaming from above. Fang's attempts at adding to the rural charm of the cottage by placing a particularly vicious looking fox's mask at the head of the stairs did not meet with suburban approval. MacDowell abandoned his wife and thundered to his children's rescue. "For God's sake, is that all!" he bellowed.

"It's horrible, I'll never sleep here," his daughter shrieked. He tugged at the offending article, which proved surprisingly determined to retain its position before suddenly coming free so that he dropped it. It bounced and rolled down the stairs narrowly led by the yelling children. There was a crash as they knocked their mother aside in their panic to escape. The fox mask bounced over his prostrate wife and the slamming of the front door added poignancy to his wife's hysterical sobbing. MacDowell headed downstairs again, reckoning there was little point in unpacking the car. He stepped carefully over his wife where she lay at the foot of the stairs rapidly developing a black eye and, kicking the leering mask, its short burst of energy had lent it a strangely perverted smirk, went to the car for the first aid box. It took several minutes to persuade his children to unlock the doors.

While the cottage guests were settling in, Fang raised a glass to Alice. "Well, I never thought it would work, but that's two hundred and fifty quid you've made."

"So long as they are all right. Did you explain about the earth closet and the range?"

"Sort of. I mentioned we believed strongly in being eco friendly and that they were a bit different as a result. Anyway, I didn't want them trying to take in too much at once. If they need help they know where we are. Shall we go to the pub tonight?"

Alice smiled. "Why not, at least it's dry and warm. Stoke up so we can have a bath and we'll get away while they're settling in. I'm sure they will like the peace and quiet." Fang felt life was improving as he rediscovered that Alice was slim and shapely when not wearing three layers of clothing to offset the chill damp that infested Bleakhope Hall.

As they frolicked in the steam filled bathroom, the MacDowells were discovering the true charm of rural living in the form of their holiday cottage. The elderly range in the kitchen proved impossible to light using firelighters on the peat that Fang had provided. The onset of dusk caused the variety of rodents that had long regarded the cottage as their own property to emerge and behave with a charming innocence regarding humans that was quite lost on Mrs MacDowell and her daughter. "A Rat! A Rat! On the Table! Kill it!" The rat, showing unexpected familiarity, appeared to wink at MacDowell as he advanced, nonchalantly dodged the chair leg he wielded and sauntered out of the door. While his wife and daughter sobbed in one another's arms, MacDowell looked wildly at his son. "Where the hell are you going? Stay and help me."

"Help do what? Repair the chair you broke or chase the mice that have climbed into the groceries?" As MacDowell lunged at the bag that issued rustles and squeaks, his son sauntered to the door. "I'm going to the loo, all right?" His return in under two minutes completed the domestic scene. The rest of the family stood in a strange tableau. Mother and daughter clung together, hysterics momentarily stilled while his father crouched transfixed over the remains of the groceries that he had cudgelled with the chair leg to an amorphous mass mixed pinkly with shrew, mouse and rat.

"What the bloody hell," his father began but stopped when something, preferably unidentifiable, slithered down his son's face and fell softly onto the floor. In a strangely quiet, unemotional, voice his son announced.

"I fell into the earth closet, then the outbuilding collapsed while I was escaping and I fell into the pile behind it with everything on top of me. His family moved as one towards the door and cleaner air. As they passed him, still in that unearthly voice he announced, "The biggest rats you've ever seen live in the earth closet."

Fang and Alice were walking down the drive towards the village and its solitary bar when the sound of a speeding vehicle came from behind. They just had time to leap onto the verge as the MacDowells passed. There was a momentary glimpse of Mrs MacDowell rocking to and fro in the front passenger seat clutching at her face with both hands, while her son appeared to be tearing his clothes off, a fact confirmed as a pair of incredibly soiled underpants flew out of the car window and landed in front of them, before the car sped from view.

"Little bugger must have a stomach upset," Fang had time to remark before a ghastly, eldritch scream sounded through the gloaming. On and on it rang, true in pitch and increasing in volume. Fang and Alice gazed wildly around and saw the MacDowells' daughter, white faced and staring eyed, sprinting down the drive towards them. She passed without seeming to notice them, still uttering her unearthly cry, and vanished into the gloom going well. "Could you make out what she was saying?" Fang enquired in a stunned voice.

"Sounded a bit like wait for me," Alice remarked. "Odd bunch though. Hope they haven't damaged the cottage." Fang laughed.

"Hard to see how. Oh well, at least they paid in advance. I'll pop down in the morning and see how they're getting on."

While Fang and Alice enjoyed a few drinks in the snug of the bar, upsetting the more traditional locals who did not approve of women in pubs, particularly those who kept indulging in cuddling and kissing their partner, the MacDowells had arrived at a motorway service station and realised they were short of a daughter. Their lamentations attracted the attention of a motorway patrol car that was pulling in for a free coffee. A minute later, MacDowell and his wife were seated in the back of the police car while their son stood forlornly, banished outside wearing a blanket provided by the increasingly angry policemen.

"You mean you leave an eight year old girl to fend for herself and force your son to go out naked and filthy? Call yourself parents?" He glared at them before picking up the microphone on the dashboard. "Delta four to Delta. Missing child, female, eight years old, probably undernourished. Abandoned somewhere on the Dumfries road."

"No, you don't understand..." began MacDowell.

"Aye, I do. So you'd better shut it until Social Services get here or I'll be having a wee word with you." The police driver rolled his broad shoulders and said nothing, his every line a rebuke. Mrs MacDowell began to weep again. "I'd get a lawyer as soon as you can, "the talkative constable announced. "You'll need one when this gets out. Eh, James?"

"Aye," replied his taciturn colleague. An ashen-faced MacDowell listened to the search for his daughter on the car speaker and stared blankly at the bright lights of the forecourt. How the hell could he explain this? His life was ruined. When his wife turned on him screaming, "

You and your bloody holiday!" he knew his marriage had also gone belly up. The curse of the Fangs fluttered unseen above the police car then winged south.

Sonya Birtle sat slumped in her armchair in her London flat, leafing through a copy of the Evening Standard. She had often thought of the Bleakhope Estate and what might have been if only Fang had managed to live long enough. Strangely, she had changed her lifestyle since that day and the last few months had seen her living a comparatively solitary existence. Due to a dramatic reduction in late and disturbed nights, she had taken no time off for so long that she had accrued a considerable leave entitlement. Idly, she wondered what to do and where to go. She was bored of her work and her colleagues and knew that a decent break would make the office at least acceptable on her return. She was riffling through the paper, wishing she had bought a magazine or even a book on the way home, when she spotted the advertisement. "ENJOY BED & BREAKFAST WITH A DIFFERENCE – STAY AT BLEAKHOPE CASTLE." A telephone number was listed and she felt it must be a sign. She dialled but there was no answer as Fang and Alice were enjoying themselves at their local. Deciding to book in the morning, she packed in preparation of leaving at lunchtime the next day.

The following afternoon saw her swinging onto the M6 northbound and singing to herself. The girl she had spoken to on the phone had seemed decent enough and had warned that the rooms available were not exactly modern. Sonya had not informed her that this came as no surprise. Being a modern girl she had felt an affinity for Bleakhope despite the abrupt end to her last visit. A more attuned ancestor would have sensed the malevolence and hate that emanated from the old tower and kept well away. Lacking perception, she did not.

Alice was desperately cleaning one of the bedrooms in the hope of making it habitable. Fang had returned from trying to check on the MacDowells to announce that they had obviously left after trying to wreck the place. "I know it's a dump, but they've played merry hell with the earth closet and seem to have a thing about taxidermy. And they seem to have carried out a pagan sacrifice using rodents. Peculiar people. You got the cheque cashed all right?" Alice was too busy to pay much attention but affirmed that the cheque had cleared. "Oh well, so long as they don't ask for their money back we'll be ok." Obtaining reimbursement was the last thing on the MacDowells minds. Gaining their freedom from police custody and their children back from Social Services was very much at the forefront of their thoughts. Unfortunately the duty solicitor did not appear very hopeful. Also, his advice in requesting Protective Custody as bail was sure to be refused and prisoners did not appreciate child abusers was frankly terrifying.

"But we love them!" Screamed Tanya MacDowell. "At least I do, I don't know about him. This whole ghastliness was his idea." MacDowell goggled at her as the solicitor sighed.

"Are you sure what you are saying? Do you wish to give evidence against your husband?"

"Yes!" she announced firmly.

"You bitch, I'll kill you!" MacDowell was dragged fighting from the interview room by the custody officer. The solicitor took a deep breath, as did the interviewing officer.

"Right, Mrs MacDowell, what happened?"

Sonya Birtle was surprised to realise how happy she felt as she approached Bleakhope Hall. When she braked to a stop and got

35

out, she felt vaguely as if she had come home. Hauling her bags from the boot of the car, she marched to the great door, which opened in front of her. A willowy red head welcomed her. "You must be Miss Birtle. Do come in. I am afraid that we are still disorganised but you said you didn't mind," she trailed off hopefully.

"Not at all. I love the place," Sonya replied disconcertingly.

"Oh, have you been here before?" Sonya prevaricated not wishing to let on that she might be said to have caused the previous Fang's death. "Just once, briefly. Carrying out research." Once Sonya had been shown her room, they gravitated to the kitchen.

"Warmest place in the house and you'll want a cup of tea I'm sure. How long are you hoping to stay?" Sonya admitted that she was not sure yet and took the proffered tea. The entrance of Fang led to further conversation and they rapidly realised that they all knew London better than the estate.

"Bloody hard to make it pay though," remarked Fang. "Tried holiday lets but they weren't a big success and you were the only response to our B and B advert." He paused before hastily adding, "Yet, that is." Sonya smiled reassuringly and then had a sudden idea. Its ramifications were enormous although none of the three realised this at the time.

"Why not use the place for management training?" She remembered her conversation with the former Fang. "I mean, the reivers seemed to be very clear on goals and team work. Why not base it on that?"

"Training? Management Training? We don't know anything about that," responded Fang.

"But I do," replied Sonya feeling suddenly useful. "I am a trainer in the city. Everyone's looking for something new, believe me."

Fang and Alice looked at one another. "But we've no accommodation suitable..." Fang stopped speaking for a moment as several ideas flitted through his mind. "I suppose they would want to live authentically, rough cottages and the like?"

"Oh yes, veracity is important. We should plan this properly, got some paper?" They sat late that night drafting up a team building and management training course to be based on the estate. Rapidly, the ideas evolved to utilising the famed loyalty and will to

36

win of the original Riding families. The trainees would live on the estate and role play at lifting cattle, guarding herds and even being at feud with one another.

"Bound to pull them together," remarked Fang with uncanny presentiment. The wine flowed and their laughter turned harsher as they talked. Outside a still night had fallen and the old tower seemed to hunch as if listening intently to discussions on how to bring back the old days continued.

Chapter 5

John Wear and Alison Sweetness sat opposite one another and gazed moodily into their respective lattes. So far, their respective searches had uncovered nothing in the form of training that might conceivably be called innovative let alone a paradigm. Having consistently seen each other at every seminar, launch and exhibition that had the slightest connection with training over the last three weeks, they had finally condescended to speak to one another. Rapidly, as their respective searches had yielded nothing that might safeguard their positions, their sinking morale had led them to meet regularly for coffee and now their day began with an early breakfast to compare each other's lack of progress. Due to their approach in their respective work places, they lacked anyone else to lend a friendly ear or to make suggestions. Indeed, it was fortunate for their plummeting morale that at least they knew someone else in a similar position as those they had belittled or annoyed were actively asking awkward questions at inopportune moments such as the Coretec coffee break, or running a book on how long they would last. It was generally agreed in Fireflow that the Sweetness looks had helped her stave off execution to date but, as she had heard echoing along the tiled corridors last night, the odds on her surviving past Friday had dropped to two to one. This was not how they had individually seen their future.

Sweetness straightened from her slump. "Right, anything in the papers today that might possibly be of any use?"

Wear started from a miserable daydream of a blighted CV. "No. Same as usual. Mind you I haven't been through them all yet. Seems a bit pointless," he trailed off despondently.

"No, look, we've got to keep trying. It shouldn't be that hard for God's sake. You can't give up now, I'd be on my own." Wear gazed at her in surprise. Somehow he had always felt that Alison Sweetness preferred to be on her own. He found this sudden vulnerability appealing.

"All right, we won't give up yet. Let's review it all again. Team building..."

"With a difference," she interrupted.

"Exactly, that's what we are looking for, different training. Then we can show the bastards." Wear gave a half smile and picked at the pile of newspapers on the table in front of him. "No, no, Reiver Training? Bollocks!"

"Just a minute," Sweetness interrupted him. "What did you say?"

"Reiver Training, I mean what the hell is that?"

"Don't know. Let me have a look." Wear spun the paper round and Sweetness lent forward to his immediate pleasure. "Stop leching," Sweetness told him without looking up. After a quick scan of the article she looked up with a smile. "This could be just what we are looking for." Wear gave up feeling vaguely resentful at Sweetness' instruction to stop letching.

"Oh yes?" The past three weeks had added cynicism to his personal traits.

"Yes! What do both our lords and masters love more than anything?"

"Trying to destroy each other."

"Exactly, and this would let them do just that – all we need to do is give them a steer."

"What are you suggesting?" he asked suddenly concentrating.

"Well, listen to this. If it doesn't fit everything we have promised and let them literally beat hell out of each other, nothing does." She suddenly giggled. "We need to plan this really carefully. Come on." She stood up abruptly and picked up her handbag and laptop. "Grab that paper," she instructed. Surprised by her sudden decision he followed meekly.

"Where are we going?"

"Where I think best," she replied and headed for the exit.

Sonya Birtle had used her intimate knowledge, in the widest sense of the word, with regard to the business editors of the quality press to ensure that the concept of Reiver Team Building and Management Training received maximum exposure. The tag lines ran along the lines of "Innovative"! "Challenging"! and "Designed to identify your future leaders within days"! On closer reading, it quickly became apparent that the training would be expensive, time consuming and likely to lead to high insurance claims from staff. The need to have at least some experience of riding also served to dissuade all but the most foolish or wealthy from further investigation. Through an extended and intimate reminiscence on an enjoyable shared evening with one city editor whose proprietor was renowned for his hypocritical views on the peccadilloes of others, she had managed to obtain both payment for the article and preferential rates for the concurrent advertisement. It had been with a merry chuckle that she had agreed that there was no need to send the photographs she had taken at the time with the then enthusiastic participation of the editor to the paper's web site. "And you will send the cheque for the article ASAP, darling?" She had giggled again. "Well, you get a story, some advertising revenue and a promise I will get in touch as soon as I get back to town. No need to be like that. Byeee!" She smiled at Fang and Alice. "Well, that went alright didn't it? We can use the money to set things up at this end."

Fang glanced at Alice then back at Sonya. "You sure about this? I mean there is no money here and…"

Sonya merely smiled. "Feed and house me just now and pay me consultancy fees when the money comes in." She viewed their doubtful faces. "It will you know, you wouldn't believe how gullible the business community can be. If it's in the papers it must be good. Just wait."

Wear was finding it hard to concentrate on what Alison Sweetness was telling him regarding how this new training idea would dig them both out of the mire. He was only too aware of her close proximity, the tantalising glimpses of her naked body that occasionally swam into view and both his overheated and overexcited condition both of which he knew were plainly apparent. She must have deliberately given him to small a towel. Alison Sweetness was too busy working out how to ensure that they presented mutually supportive plans to their respective Chief execs to notice his discomfort. She loved the sauna; it was the only place that even faintly resembled her memories of Queensland. Hot, steamy conditions were her natural habitat she felt and relaxed for a moment before forcing herself to concentrate on tactics once more. "Right" she announced. "We know what motivates the bastards so the solution is simple."

"Is it?" Wear queried.

"Of course, we just let slip that we know the other's company is going to attend Reiver training and they will immediately plan to go at the same time to prove they are better. We just need to play up the competitive nature of it all, you know, open competition, winner takes all...just like the old days from what I have read"

Wear frowned, "But won't they realise we've been talking? You know what that would mean." He ran a hand over his sweating face and tried to concentrate. His companion shifted and he found it even harder to focus on their planning. Alison Sweetness was well aware of how she was distracting him and intended to continue doing so until he fell in line with her thinking. With another minute movement she ensured that yet more of her upper thighs became visible.

"These damned towels are so constricting," she announced inconsequentially. Wear gulped and sweated some more. She decided that he was ready to fall in line. "What we do is get more facts from this Reiver Training bunch, write up reports and then tell them that we know that the other's company has already signed up because this Reiver lot couldn't help bragging. Then no one connects us, they both concentrate on the thought of beating the other and they will overrule any opposition from the staff."

Wear thought this over. "You know, it would work, I mean, they'd be so busy thinking of the pluses that they'd ignore everything else. Brilliant!"

She stood up and let her towel drop to the floor. "I am." She gently dodged his lunge and threw the door open. "A cold plunge will help," she informed him looking pointedly at his groin area and strolled out.

The telephone call asking for more details at first stunned then galvanised the inhabitants of Bleakhope. "Details on Reiver Management Training and Team Building? Yes, certainly. Your address? Get a pen, a pen! Sorry, right you were saying." Alice covered the receiver. "For god's sake, stop making such a row. We want to appear professional." She uncovered the phone again. "A pleasure, we will get literature and a quotation off to you by the end of the week. How many people would you like to attend?" Her mouth dropped open and she gazed in wonder at the receiver. "I'm sorry, I didn't quite catch that." She gazed wonderingly at Fang

41

and Sonya who gazed back with equal disbelief. The disembodied voice seemed strangely loud in the suddenly silent kitchen. "Probably thirty." Alice took a grip of herself and avoided squeaking in response. "Oh good," she managed. "That will help." She allowed the caller to assume that she meant the numbers would facilitate training not that the fees would mean that they would survive. "I will get things organised now. Thank you, bye." She put the phone down then hugged Fang and Sonya together. They were still grouped together in a celebratory huddle when the phone rang again. They looked at it and back at each other in wonder before Alice picked it up once more. "Bleakhope Hall. Details on Reiver management Training and Team Building?" Two minutes later the kitchen witnessed a strange, primal jig of celebration as they whooped and danced around the room. The elderly spaniel that Mrs Burns had returned as soon as they had taken up residence, made its unvarying comment on the unusual, and left ahead of the stench.

"Christ Almighty!" Fang gasped, and the jig petered out amongst oaths and the flinging open of windows.

Later, Fang called a management meeting to consider the best way forward. "What the hell do we do now? I mean, we need to send them something and then, what do we charge? Christ!" The sense of euphoria fled and he looked to the women.

"Well," Alice announced. "We fit something together, I'll get a local printer to rush us two brochures for proofreading and we'll get them off. We can order more and pay for them later. I'll get dressed up before I go in. Now what should we charge them?" To Fang's surprise the girls saw only solutions not problems. As various fees were bandied around he started to rootle under the sink. "You drank it all," Alison informed him before turning her attention back to Sonya. Finally, they agreed a charge of eleven hundred pound per head reduced for a block booking to one thousand pounds for a week's training. Then they got down to drafting a seemingly sensible training plan. As soon as this was completed, Alice rushed upstairs and searched furiously through her clothes to try and find something that looked vaguely tweedy and monied.

Finally she reappeared wearing an old jacket and jeans tucked into knee length boots that looked somehow acceptable. Sonya looked her up and down. "Neat, here, put on my pearls, you might as well look the part." Fang and Sonya watched her rattle off down the drive waving furiously before disappearing from sight.

"Right," Sonya announced, "when are you going to organise horses? I mean we can't have Reiver training on foot can we?" Dumbly, Fang shook his head. The women seemed to be running the show and he found it uncomfortable.

By the time Alice returned clutching her papers and announcing the printers would have run off several samples by the morning, Fang had obtained a copy of the local paper from the village and was carefully checking the animal section. "What are you doing?" she enquired.

"Looking for bloody horses," he answered bitterly. "They seem to be more expensive than cars and everyone wants a loving home for their little treasure." He slumped back in his chair and the Fang scowl turned his features vaguely evil. He pondered for a few moments, then sat up. "Let me see the agricultural section." He read carefully for two minutes then looked up with a grin. "It says here that Sand Dance stables are finding the drop in tourism bad for business. That means they're on their uppers like us. Why don't we make them an offer to keep the ponies and exercise them until things improve. We can say that we want to offer riding with our holiday homes and rent them for the summer. If things are going well we can buy them at a knock down price. Come on, let's go and visit." Alice smiled sweetly and followed him out the door.

The owners of Sand Dance stables listened carefully to Fang's offer while clutching hands. The rural idyll had gone horribly wrong and now all they wanted was to get the ponies off their hands and let the fields for grazing. They seemed a pleasant young couple and they even engendered a moment's conscience despite the desperation of the situation. "Look, are you sure you need all of them? I mean" he broke off suddenly as his wife kicked him on the ankle. "What sort of fee were you thinking of?" Fang, who had noticed the kick, chose to misunderstand the question.

"Oh, we aren't greedy, are we darling? No, something like fifty a week. Would that be fair?" The negotiations paused momentarily as the Sand Dancers hissed furiously at one another before turning back with haggard looks on their faces.

"Well, um, we'd rather hoped that you would pay us, so, um."

Fang gave an ancestral smile and they quailed visibly. "Ah, I see." He paused for a moment. "Tell you what, we'll look after the blacksmith and feed and so forth and when you get straightened out we can look again at fees for keep." It was only once they had shaken hands on the deal and Fang and Alice had driven away promising to return in the morning to collect the ponies that the Sand Dancers felt perhaps they had missed something.

"At least I won't need to look at the little bastards," he unfeelingly remarked to his tearful wife as they headed indoors.

The next day saw a further flurry of activity at Bleakhope. Alice rushed off to the printers to collect the promised samples, Fang visited his tenants to ensure that he had enough trailers and livestock containers to move the ponies and Sonya pored over the estate map to identify areas to locate the teams. By the end of the day, Fang had found his newly discovered skill at hard bargaining honed through dealing with recalcitrant tenant farmers who had no intention of doing something for nothing. Sonya had found two widely separated groups of farm buildings that at least would provide a base for the teams to be located. Both would, however, require an immense amount of work to make the most basic of bunkhouses with minimal facilities. She was rather surprised by Fang's disregard for the difficulties that this might cause. "Well, we'll tell them that it's all part of the training experience, reward them with food and hot water if they perform tasks well." Alice and Sonya exchanged glances, he was beginning to worry them with this new, harder approach. Where previously he had been somewhat hesitant in his approach to problems, now he just seemed to brush them aside and any objections with them. His next statement reaffirmed their concerns. "What's the stabling like? Can't let the ponies suffer too much."

"Better than the sleeping accommodation," she responded.

"Right, tomorrow we put together bunks out of any wood we can find, the promotional material states that we are recreating the lifestyle of the reivers to ensure the training is sufficiently authentic to ensure they learn the value of team work and decision making doesn't it? Well, we'd be cheating them if we made it too comfortable."

"There are degrees of comfort," Sonya murmured. Fang chose not to hear her.

"So, we get the paperwork off to them tonight, ensure that they pay a booking fee of say ten percent and use the money to dress things up a bit. Oh, and cattle, I've discovered that you get a subsidy for native breeds so I'm going to get some Belted Galloways for them to chase. I read they are fit little buggers so they should run around fine." Somewhat relieved the girls agreed with his suggestions.

Fang and Alice walked down to the village that evening to catch the early mail collection in the morning and have a couple of drinks in the pub. As they passed the old tower, a cold breeze stirred the branches of the trees and swirled around them momentarily. Alice shivered and clutched Fang's arm while he gazed up at the night sky and then looked south as if he was watching something flying overhead. "Well, that's done," he announced as they entered the pub a few minutes later. Back in its cloak of trees, Bleakhope Tower suddenly seemed to form a harder, more distinct, silhouette.

Chapter 6

An air of sullen expectation hung pall like over the Bleakhope estate. Alice and Sonya were still concerned as to the incredibly basic living quarters that Fang felt were suitable for the course attendees to use. Fang was disappointed in their reaction, sore and tired after organising the buildings and the delivery of the cattle. All three were concerned that Coretec and Fireflow would take one look and vanish south while issuing writs for false promises, and the cattle were just awaiting a chance for revenge on the bungling humans who had brought them down from the moors and away from their mothers. Altogether it created that ambience that had ensured Bleakhope was never high on the list of popular visitor destinations even during the various wars with England. True to form, the spaniel sloped quietly into view sensing that something was going to occur. Finally, Fang felt that he had to break the mood.

"Look, I'm sure it will be all right. After all, we've put a lot of effort into things and you two have pulled together a brilliant package." This statement was greeted by a long silence broken only by a strange noise from the spaniel's direction that could be loosely interpreted as a snigger. Realising that it had attracted attention to itself it moved deeper into the shadows by the back door. Fang cursed under his breath, the cattle lowed menacingly in the distance and Alice announced she was putting on the kettle. Sonya felt that she should give them some space and wandered off in the direction of the old tower.

A few minutes later, Fang clutched the mug of coffee Alice had brought him and the pair wandered aimlessly to look down the drive. Suddenly an eldritch screech sounded from the tower and Fang spilled his coffee in surprise. Sonya was waving her arms furiously and shouting incoherently. "What has happened now?" Fang enquired of Alice before bellowing up at the wind-milling figure. "Has the roof given way?" With an obvious effort, Sonya made herself call more coherently.

"They're coming, cars, quick!"

Fang gazed up at her in something akin to horror. "What, here?"

"Yes, lots of cars!" "Get down here, you are meant to be dressed in character and welcoming them with a drink. Run." Alice sprinted off towards the house and a wail announced Sonya had taken a quicker route down the spiral staircase than she had planned. The first cars crept cautiously into the fold yard and two young men got out and gazed about with a worried air. Fang strolled over, trying to give the impression that he knew what he was doing. "Afternoon. Good journey?" Without waiting for a reply he turned to look at the next car pulling in. "Best thing to do is take the car and drive through that gate, take your luggage and come back here. Ok?" Still silent, the two Coretec staff merely nodded and turned to obey. Cheered by this ready acquiescence, Fang approached the next arrivals and despatched them to park their car. Soon the fold yard was bustling as people arrived, removed vehicles and reappeared clutching various amounts of luggage. The arrival of two identical black Range Rovers whose drivers got out and pointedly turned their backs on one another alerted Fang that Mickley and Galphay had arrived. An attempt to repeat his mantra led to Galphay throwing his keys to a hovering acolyte together with an instruction not to scratch it, while Mickley inclined his head in his direction before calling over an assistant.

"I wonder if you would mind moving, the, ah," he waved a languid arm. Fang noticed with interest that each approach had a similar effect as the vehicles were removed and luggage returned at incredible speed.

"Right everyone, into the barn," Fang ordered and, to his amazement, they did as instructed.

Once in the building, the throng split ostentatiously into two and formed around their Managing Directors. Fang sensed a definite atmosphere that seemed stronger than that engendered by natural competitiveness. Both groups looked comparatively young and reasonably fit with the exception of two or three on either side who limped or had arms in slings. He was not to know that this was as a direct result of trying to learn to ride in the short time available before attending the training exercise at Bleakhope. If he had been aware of this fact, he would have realised that they not unnaturally blamed him as the cause of their physical discomfort. Being ignorant, he merely thought that they were unpleasantly hostile for no good reason. This was not a state that could be attributed to either Mickley or Galphay. Their hostility was both mutual and directly attributable. They glared at one another, made bitter little asides to their close lieutenants and generally indulged themselves. They were momentarily distracted by the arrival of Alice and Sonya dressed in kirtles and long skirts in the fashion of the sixteenth century. Before they could work themselves up further, their supporters took the opportunity to separate them by gently blocking them in so that they could no longer see their enemy through the close grouped bodies. "What the hell is that ghastly fellow doing here!"

This was immediately followed by a snarled request to, "Let me settle that bugger now!" Fang realised that there was something going on that he did not understand and decided it was time to take control.

"Ladies and gentlemen, please sit down and I will explain in a little detail what the training is all about." He waited while his audience milled around until they realised that he meant them to sit on the straw bales scattered around the barn. "That's the way," he announced brightly when one or two sat but then he realised that the two groups were ensuring that they were as far apart as possible. "This is meant to be training based on friendly competition," he announced. Galphay hawked and spat loudly by way of response and Mickley sniffed. Fang sighed; he just knew this was going to be a long afternoon, before stepping into the centre of the barn.

"Right, a few words on what to expect, housekeeping and so on and then I will explain what we hope to achieve. Ok?" Taking the lead from their respective Managing Directors, both sides observed a stony silence. Fang decided to try and ease the tension. "While I talk you should have a drink, after all it's been a long journey for you all." He waited while Alice and Sonya scurried around the room carrying large jugs of home brew. "Just to get you in the historical mood, there is only ale to drink or water." He ignored the muttering from the occasional teetotaller. "Both teams will be living in old farm buildings that have been converted into bunkhouses while you are here. These are your bases. You will also find that there are stabling for your ponies and grazing for both them and some cattle. The reason for this will become obvious shortly. The idea behind the training is to try and learn from the Border Reivers, extended families or clans who stuck together against all and sundry and made their living by reiving, or stealing cattle. They also tended to have blood feuds and ran protection rackets but we won't be doing that!" His chuckle died as his audience viewed him in stony silence. "Well, as I was saying, we believe there are valuable lessons to be learnt for modern businesses in an increasingly competitive environment through studying and actively following the precepts of the Reivers. Clear goal setting, an awareness of the cost of failure, the benefits of a tight knit team and, perhaps most importantly, individual responsibility and decision making. While you learn all that we also think you'll have fun."

Fang continued in a similar vein for some time but rapidly concluded his speech was being listened to at best in a desultory fashion and probably ignored virtually completely. He paused and tried to determine when he had lost his audience and decided it was when he had strayed onto the training speech that Sonya had so carefully coached him in delivering. By way of experiment, he returned to the lifestyle of the reivers.

"Strangely, they did not go in for robbing innocent travellers but concentrated their efforts against the local population on both sides of the border, raiding, weakening the opposition by any means possible and sometimes this lead to outright warfare." He stopped and observed them closely. Once more they hung on his words. He suppressed a shiver. "They were a product of the times in which they lived and, as you are products of your times, we are looking for slightly different results."

A loud yawn greeted this attempt to lead them back into the present day and management training and team building. Realising that he was getting absolutely nowhere, Fang decided to try and make them uncomfortable. "Now, before we go any further, you are allowed three changes of clothing, no cars and no mobiles, or any other electronic devices. Oh, no cameras either!" he managed to bellow over the rising crescendo of protests.

Ten minutes later, a dishevelled Fang glared at the tattered figures of Sonya and Alice. "For God's sake Sonya, you're flashing your boobs and Alice, you've lovely legs but they wore their skirts long in those days not micro." They stared angrily back at him before turning back to face the crowd again. "It's good to see such a team approach to resisting change," he announced, "but unfortunately you are defeating the whole idea of the training. You will live as they did in the sixteenth century borders. No success, no food, and certainly no communication with the outside world. Now for the last time, put everything that is not allowed into the labelled sacks you have been given and we will store them securely for the week. Gentlemen," he addressed Mickley and Galphay. "It is your time and money they are wasting. I will add the ladies wrecked attire to your respective invoices." His words had a remarkable effect and very shortly Alice and Sonya were standing over two separate heaps of possessions.

Wear and Sweetness had both relaxed slightly having used the opportunity of the group search and concomitant resistance to exchange a few words. Both were aware of the dislike in which they were held and knew that this antipathy was only going to strengthen with the imposition of strict training rules.

"Before we show you to your team bases, the girls will pass everyone a folder explaining the basic premise behind the training." Fang paused. "Winning." He smiled wolfishly. "Win and you eat, lose and you wait another day. You'll find that it concentrates your minds on the essentials of each task. I will visit both camps once you have had a chance to settle in and get used to your ponies. You'll need them" The muttered groans at these announcements gave Fang considerable pleasure that he did his best to disguise.

"I know, but it is only for a week," he falsely sympathised. "Now, you have about three hours before I come and brief you on the first challenges so please follow the ladies who will take you to your respective bases." He watched the two groups jostle one another as they left and tried to ignore the muttered threats that hung heavy in the air. He was sure it was just his imagination that gave their voices harsher accents redolent with menace.

When the girls returned, Fang had made tea and put a bottle of whisky on the kitchen table. "Bloody hell, Sonya, are all training courses like this lot?" Sonya gazed at him and wordlessly shook her head before slumping into a chair. Alice lent against the table and they both looked silently at Fang. "What? What's wrong?" he demanded defensively.

"We've been pinched, kicked, groped and cursed and all we did was try and get them to follow some pretty simple rules and all you do is threaten to invoice them for our clothes!" Alice exploded. "When I showed them what you jokingly call the bunk house they threatened to beat me up." Sonya looked up from where she was huddled over a mug of tea.

"I felt sorry for them at first. Now I hope it rains. Then we'll see who looks like a tramp." Absent-mindedly she tried to push her left breast back into the remains of her dress and contemplated the effect of a heavy downpour on the residents of the old farm steadings. They had been too busy being horrible to realise the roofs were full of holes. "Bastards," she announced before falling silent once more. Fang smiled quietly to himself. The girls glared at him and he broke into a chuckle.

"There you are the two of you, cursing me for not doing more to get them back for what they've done to you. What neither of you have realised is that you can stand back and watch revenge being carried out on your behalf and we won't have to lift a finger." They stared at him. "Look, they obviously hate each other, I bet they land up beating hell out of each other and what's more, they'll be paying us good money to do it." He sniggered nastily. "If it makes you feel better we'll give them a night exercise to get team building off to a good start. Now, you made sure they all signed exemptions for any damages or injuries resulting from training?" Sonya nodded emphatically. "Right, just relax and watch what happens," he laughed again and this time Alice and Sonya joined in.

At the Fireflow homestead, the staff were not happy and making it obvious. The Director of Development was gazing in horror at what Alice had tried to pass off as sleeping quarters. "How the hell·could anyone sleep here?" he enquired plaintively. "I mean, look at it. I wouldn't put a cow in here." On cue, one of the Galloways bellowed mournfully from outside.

51

"For Christ's sake what the fuck was that?" shrieked his assistant, a delicate soul whose idea of an energetic weekend was walking to the corner shop to buy a paper.

"It was a cow, dear boy. A cow." Mickley appeared undisturbed by the squalor for which he was paying. "Surely you can recognise a cow? Now, this should be interesting. At least it will be a change from the humdrum of normal life. Hmm?" To everyone's surprise his Operations Director disagreed vehemently.

"It will be bloody hell! No hot water, only beer to drink and I bet that's because there is no safe water supply and has anyone found a cooker? I thought not," he concluded darkly. Mickley looked at him.

"You seem a trifle over wrought my boy," Mickley admonished him with a steely look. "The important thing is not a few days discomfort but to humiliate that shower that have also turned up. Now get sorted out before they provide us with our first challenge. Don't want to be caught napping." The Director of Operations muttered it was unlikely anyone could nap in this place but Mickley chose not to hear him. Disconsolately they shuffled out to look at the ponies finding the interior of their temporary home too depressing to remain.

Over at the Coretec steading, although equally unhappy with their circumstances, the complaints of the throng were drowned out by the haranguing of their leader. "Stop poncing around and listen up! We are not going to be beaten by that sod and his hangers on so get thinking. Now I want a coffee." His Personal Assistant took great pleasure in informing him that there was none.

"You can always have a beer but I wouldn't drink the water. The cattle seem to share the trough with us." She quietly moved back into the crowd while Galphay raged impotently. When he realised that his outburst was losing effect he suddenly calmed.

"Right, how are we going to beat those buggers?" Disconcertingly, he was met by silence. "Right, you dozy sods, go and check the horses. And be ready!" His workforce drifted outside and he heard their disgust clearly through the holes in the walls.

"Get me a coffee! Time he realised what this is going to be like."

"Liked the crack about the water."

"I'm afraid it's true."

"Oh God!" The last exclamation was explained by the personal assistant blundering into the old midden behind the steading and a rich smell of old manure roiled into the building. Galphay moved rapidly into the open.

"Right, let's get our act together. Who's looked at the beasts yet, hey?"

Gradually, the enthusiasm and will of their respective employers caused both sides to start developing ideas to overcome the opposition. Fireflow's Marketing Department started muttering about strategic aims while the Director of Sales exhorted his team to identify their goals. Under the Coretec regime, the Finance department who had been counselling caution and the harbouring of resources were shouted down by Development who felt there were opportunities for rapidly taking over the Fireflow cattle. Galphay was cheered visibly by this positive attitude and threw himself into further encouraging his troops.

"Wait 'til they give us our first challenge, then we'll show the buggers!"

Mickley was equally bullish in an understated way.

"Just put our hearts and minds into it fully and we will prevail. Think of the team!" The post room thought of Spurs who they supported to a man and shook their heads, unable to think of any inspiration there.

Chapter 7

Fang ensured that he had Sonya and Alice with him when he visited the trainees. "Look, they need to see a united front. You can't let them know that you've been upset. We need to remind them we are the trainers. Anyway, we'll convince them how it's all results based. No win, no food then go and get some fish and chips." Alice smiled wanly. "Look, I promised you that you'd get your own back. Wait until I've stirred them up and see what happens!" Sonya giggled despite herself. To be honest, being roughly handled and half stripped by an uncaring mob of strangers was strangely exciting. So long as she wasn't expected to put up with it again she was happy to retain the memory for further consideration when she finally got to bed. Alice merely loathed both companies and wanted to see them suffer. She had found nothing interesting in the experience and desired to only to see certain people looking extremely foolish in as public a setting as possible.

Both groups had lost interest in planning the defeat of the opposition as basic instincts to ensure their survival had crept in. They had started ensuring that they had shelter and warmth. This led to a considerable amount of dust and confusion as the female element on both sides tried to clean the living areas.

"Bloody hell!" Galphay announced and, waving his arms blundered into the open air. Across the estate, Mickley was virtually mirroring his actions without the expletives.

"Rather dusty," he announced, stepping into the open air. Behind him a heated discussion was breaking out between the female element and the Assistant Director of Operations on how to make their quarters more homely and welcoming. To be fair to the women, they were motivated by a wish to merely make the conditions bearable and felt that rearranging such simple things as bales of straw would create privacy and reduce draughts. For some unknown reason this offended the artistic streak in the Assistant Director.

"Think of the lines for God's sake! Why can you not grasp beauty can be practical." The response he received from the normally gentle soul who rounded on him left him momentarily speechless.

"I'll be artistically practical where I shove this bale if you don't bugger off!" He did as ordered and went to complain loudly to his immediate colleagues that the women were obviously too weak to cope with the training and were becoming emotional. While this developed into a full scale screaming match, Mickley asked why his Head of Property was not getting involved in organising the rearrangement of the building choosing instead to gaze in a daydream at the walls. He was rather taken aback by the reply.

"Actually, I'm intrigued by how the walls are still standing considering they have no founds, the degree of subsidence and their own weight not to mention that of the roof." Mickley stared. "Look, that opening there, you see it?"

"That door? Of course, what of it, man?"

"Well, it's not a door, it's a crack." After a long silence they all drifted outside while trying to appear casual. It was only when they realised the Head of Property had not joined them that they returned, He was found pouring himself a beer. When asked, he replied there was nowhere else to stay, it had lasted a few hundred years, and if he drank enough he'd stop worrying. Strangely his words were not felt to be very reassuring or in the Fireflow spirit.

Coretec, true to its famed democratic approach to decision making, were being told what to do by Galphay. When Marketing tried to remonstrate that this was hardly developing individual decision-making and responsibility, he found himself rapidly joining the human chain that was passing straw bales for the construction of a wall to fill the large hole in the front wall. "Old tosser," he muttered to a colleague from Planning. "I've a good mind to jack!"

"I wouldn't, he's looking for a victim to make an example and out here he'd probably have you stoned or flogged," Marketing goggled. "Alright, I exaggerate but he's in a foul mood and it would take years to get what you're owed out of him." They both sighed then carried on heaving bales. Once the initial blocking up work was completed, a degree of discussion broke out between the workforce. It centred on the apparently ham fisted efforts of the males to assist in making the place inhabitable in the eyes of the women present. While this shameless reversion to old-fashioned stereotyping caused outrage, the more perceptive males, mainly in the Sales team, wondered why dedicated feminists were so willing to ditch previously strongly held beliefs. A shrill whinny cut through the hubbub.

"They're scared of the horses."

"Well, that's obvious, but so am I."

"What we've got to do is overcome their objections."

"True, but we have to carefully identify them and show them the benefits of the proposition."

"Ok, I'll lead."

They strolled over to where the shrillest grouping was haranguing every male they could and the youngest salesman put his honed skills into practice. "Look, you'll never get over your fear of the nags if you don't go and work with them. It's simple!" Once they got back outside, Sales looked at their junior member who rubbed his reddening cheek. "What?" he demanded. "How was I to know she was obviously suffering from PMT?"

"Well," his director observed. "You didn't handle it quite as I taught you but I must admit she did over react."

"Bloody right. You'd think I meant to be offensive. I was only trying to help her face her fears when I said she was... oh God she's coming back." He nipped off round the corner of the steading. Almost immediately they were approached by a despondent looking Wear.

"Look guys, he wants us to show a lead and get our ponies organised." The Director of Sales sneered openly.

"Lead on. You organised this little jaunt so why don't you have all the fun. We'll watch and see how it's done."

Fireflow were astounded. As they watched the ugly scene unfold they winced and one or two even turned their backs. Well to the front, Mickley merely slightly slitted his eyes as the small tragedy he had caused was played out. Tiring of the increasingly noisy discussion over how best to make the buildings bearable, he had looked for something to underline his authority not having forgotten the earlier dissension shown by the Operations Director and the Head of Property. He had soon spotted Sweetness watching the developing fracas with a detachment that he found strangely irritating. "Now, my dear," he announced. "Enough of this home making. Get a pony saddled up and make sure they are rideable before they come and tell us what the first challenge is." Sweetness had stared at him for long seconds before turning and picking up a rope halter and saddle from the heap that Fang had dumped in a pile by the door. She threw the saddle onto the broken down dry stonewall that surrounded the steading and arranged the stirrup leathers carefully so that they crossed the saddle then shouldered the burden. The ponies, sensing that they were being viewed by a growing number of humans, bunched together and postured. As she walked quietly towards the animals, her colleagues discussed the situation noisily. "Obviously scared." "Serve the bitch right, look where she's landed us." "Pride comes before a fall." She stopped and glared back at them. Someone made a chicken noise from deep in the crowd and Sweetness flushed before turning and trudging on. The ponies had learnt survival in a hard school at a succession of riding stables and adopted their usual tactics of prancing and milling while neighing noisily. The most hard bitten character among them advanced on Sweetness who stood and watched it closely as it came up to her. She raised a tentative hand to stroke its muzzle and it bit her. "Bastard" She screamed and flew at the animal in a flurry of kicks and punches. At first the pony had fought back, rearing up and pawing the air with its front hooves but it was no match for Sweetness who continued to rain blows at it. Finally, the animal broke away only to find Sweetness pursuing it uttering shrill Antipodean oaths. It made the mistake of trying to kick her with its hind legs but she easily dodged and grasped its mane. The two figures could be seen struggling furiously in a cloud of dust before a stillness descended. The human and equine audiences gazed in stunned amazement at the scene and finally made out that Sweetness was on the pony's back. She walked the animal over to Mickley and forced him to take a step back as she was deliberately late in forcing the animal to halt. "The bastards will behave now!" she announced before forcing the pony to trot through her colleagues who scattered out of her path.

Coretec were not enjoying getting acquainted with their ponies. Disturbingly for several staff who had spent good money on riding lessons, the ponies did not seem to have learnt the same commands they had been taught. Attempts at fitting bridles and saddles had rapidly turned into a painful experience as the ponies utilised every unpleasant trick they had learnt. Realising that their would be riders were nervous as well as incompetent, the animals played on this fact, nipping, turning their hindquarters menacingly towards people, standing on toes. Soon, Coretec had retreated en masse from this equine assault and huddled together muttering to each other. Galphay was not impressed. Hiding the fact that he had been taught to ride as a boy and, indeed, often went riding at the weekend, he berated his staff. "You pathetic buggers!" He snarled at the cowed group. "They're bloody ponies, not Dobermans. Now go and get sorted." To his amazement he found himself facing a silent mutiny. As one, they stood mutely but refused to make a move no matter how he raged. Realising that his usual approach was not working, Galphay surprised them all. He turned his back on them, grabbed a head harness and bridle and marched up to the nearest pony. To their astonishment, he rapidly overcame the animal's objections and led it back to them. Giving the animal a quick shake, he passed the head rope to the nearest body and turned away to repeat the feat. By the time he had provided five ponies, his staff were paying close attention. This time he carefully talked them through the procedure and soon they found themselves dealing at least half competently with the remaining ponies. Recognising that their bluff had been called, the animals behaved. Recognising that he had better try and ensure a basic level of competence, Galphay then taught them how to saddle their potential mounts. This display of competence and involvement further unnerved his workers and they meekly followed his instructions to remove all the tack from the animals and do it again.

Fang was pleasantly surprised when he arrived at the Fireflow encampment. The ponies had witnessed the total defeat and humiliation of their leader and had meekly submitted to the bungling attempts by their would be riders to tack them up. Sweetness had herded the animals over to her colleagues, sneered eloquently if silently and ridden off. Fang found a line of ponies carefully picketed in rows in front of the steading in a fashion that he finally recognised from photographs of the Boer War. The head ropes had all been hitched to lengths of rope that were securely tied to stakes that had been hammered into the earth. Each pony was able to move within a limited area but unable to reach its neighbour. Suppressing a whistle, he walked over to the waiting crowd. "Enjoying yourselves?" He enquired brightly. Alice and Sonya stood behind him watching. In Alice's case, she was trying to identify the bastard who had pinched her backside, while Sonya was actually trying to gauge the mood of the trainees. She was left in little doubt when she noticed several Fireflow members near the back, spit in response to Fang's question. A sense of hostility hung in the air but Fang seemed oblivious. "Excellent! Right, now that you're organised I will explain the first task. What you need to do is carry out a reconnaissance tonight, on horseback, to identify the opposition's weaknesses. It will be useful later on when we give you the next set of challenges." He smiled brightly. "Now, you need to bear in mind that success means that you get food, failure means you go hungry." He was forced to speak louder over the growing muttering that had replaced the earlier sullen silence. "The idea behind the training is to learn from the Reivers techniques. Work as a team, seize opportunities either as individuals or a group, and win. To signal the start of the exercise, I will light a beacon on top of the old tower." He turned to point it out. "It will be extinguished quite quickly so keep watch so you don't miss it. The exercise ends at daylight." He turned away followed by the girls. "We'll be acting as umpires" he called, then felt it necessary to expand. "You've read all the background notes, haven't you?" They nodded and glanced at each other trying to identify who had actually done so. "Right, well, good luck." The trio left.

Coretec had followed a different approach regarding their ponies and had created a form of coral within which the animals stood, exhibiting few signs of their earlier truculence. Several staff stood looking at them and considering the night ahead. "The ponies are bad enough, what are the cattle going to be like?" One wondered.

"At least the ponies are meant to be semi domesticated ...." Another tailed off. A bellow from Galphay instructing them to get their arses inside to hear what was going off ended the musings. In a similar fashion to their Fireflow counterparts, being reminded that failure meant hunger brought out their anger and Fang left while Galphay was shouting down their objections. He had been about to ask Alice and Sonya what they thought when a voice hailed them from behind. They turned and Wear approached them.

"I just wanted to check the details as I couldn't hear for the noise back there and I will be blamed if it goes wrong." Fang smiled unpleasantly before repeating the instructions. "Right, thanks, I'll explain to the rest of them." He trotted off. Fang watched him with interest before turning to the girls.

"Well, different approaches. Who do you think will win the first round?" Alice gazed stonily back at him.

"Who cares as long as they suffer!" Fang studied her angry face.

"Look, plenty of things go wrong in the dark. We make sure we see what's going on without getting involved and you can enjoy watching them suffer!"

"And how are we going to do that?"

"I bought a night vision scope when we were in town last Thursday. It's a sod for batteries but we can use it carefully until I get some rechargeables." Both Alice and Sonya considered this information with interest and started thinking how they might use it for their own ends.

Fireflow found themselves gathered round the unlikely attraction of the office bore in the form of a programmer who had actually read all the training information and was able to provide his colleagues with a potted history of the reivers and their tactics. Mickley listened and smiled benignly while he considered how best to gain the upper hand over Galphay. When the programmer had started to repeat himself, proving that they had extracted as much information as possible, Marketing went into planning mode. They huddled together and waved their arms while talking animatedly before including their Operations colleagues in the discussion. Soon, the group were ready to explain their action plan for the opening of the Fireflow campaign. Their audience listened attentively before breaking up laughing heartily. Even Sweetness felt momentarily included when someone patted her on the shoulder and remarked how they'd soon sort that bunch out. As dusk fell Mickley drifted around arranging his staff into the various roles and groupings in accordance with Marketing's tactics. "Now, Freda, you are, um, remembering the overall strategy, hmm?" The Head of Marketing reassured him as to this point and that the tactic would go a considerable way towards achieving their strategic aim. Mickley rubbed his hands together with pleasure. "Good, good. He really is a four letter man." Marketing gazed at him. "Galphay" he said by way of explanation. She wondered momentarily if he had gone mad, surely there were eight not four letters in Galphay, before she realised what Mickley had meant. Meantime, Mickley had drifted away and was informing Sales that he saw them in the form of leading scouts. "Fit the way your minds work" he informed them "Need some sneaky blighters always willing to do the other chap. It's a dog eat dog world out there!" Sales agreed totally and added that they were just the people for the job. Satisfied that a little flattery had made sure that they had willing volunteers for the riskiest role, Mickley moved away.

Galphay was not finding matters so easy. As he had always insisted on making decisions himself, his staff had been carefully trained to not decide anything until they had his agreement and certainly not to try and be original in thought or action. His problems were exacerbated by lacking information as he had not paid attention to Fang or, indeed, having read the information sent by Fang. To his increasing frustration, his staff merely stood and looked at him waiting to be told what to do. Only Wear was willing to put his head over the parapet and even he was extremely cautious in doing so. "Come on you useless sods, ideas!"

"Well" Wear found his interjection resulted in a sudden space around him. Wear gulped then started to explain what was required following his discussion with Fang. For once he found himself listened to without criticism.

"So, what do you suggest we do" Galphay enquired. Wear took a deep breath.

"We should ride out en masse in case we bump into them. It would be more efficient if we went out a small groups and reported back, but remember that they will want to take us." He noticed the vein beating in Galphay's temple and hurriedly added "And we don't want to miss a chance if we bump into them wandering around." After an uncharacteristic moments hesitation, Galphay issued his orders.

"We go out all together and hope we find them. While we do that we can have a look at their set up" He glared at the throng. "Right, get organised and we'll get going."

As dusk fell, both camps grew noisier as the amount of ale consumed grew. This had the effect of cheering the majority and, for the first time, genuine laughter was heard. Admittedly, the drink did not have a positive effect on them all. The more naturally pessimistic merely slumped lower in spirit and told all who would listen that the training was a waste of time and could only get worse. Largely they were ignored or teased, but one unfortunate from Coretec was overheard by Galphay. This led to a particularly memorable verbal explosion that awed even the most hardened Coretec employee. It also had the effect of ensuring that no one would dare to disagree or even question Galphay openly for the next few hours. This was to work to their detriment. More immediately, the general response was to have several more drinks as quickly as possible. While Coretec were endeavouring to drown their sorrows, Fireflow grew more confident as the amount they drank grew and, in turn, their attitude became more aggressive. The tone of laughter grew harsher and the banter more vicious. The Fireflow personnel started to suggest ever more aggressive ways of not just defeating but destroying Coretec. Mickley was delighted by this and happily encouraged the wilder spirits. This open support of his views on Coretec and more particularly Galphay was just what he wanted to hear. By full dark, neither contingent could be described as sober.

By the time Fang stumbled cursing to the top of the old tower to light his signal beacon having broken his hand torch when he tripped on the uneven steps, clouds had rolled in to intermittently cover the moon and both sets of trainees had reached a pitch of aggression and recklessness. When he finally managed to light the beacon, he not only signalled the start of the first training exercise, but also kindled a conflagration that was to scorch all who lived in the vicinity of Bleakhope.

Chapter 8

As the beacon guttered then flared into life, both encampments were galvanised into action. The groups moved almost as one, some staggering slightly as the ale made itself felt. Fireflow were motivated by aggression and belief in their plans, Coretec in a mass desire to escape any criticism from Galphay who had been drinking solidly. While Fang stumbled around the top of the tower trying not to fall down the stairwell or off the roof having lost his night vision while the beacon burned, the trainees approached their ponies. Hearing Galphay's voice, the ponies stood shivering and allowed their riders to saddle up without hindrance. True to their normal approach, Coretec rushed to saddle their mounts and, without a moments hesitation, swung onto their backs. Someone pulled aside the branches that had been used to block the entrance to the stockade and they thundered into the night in a solid phalanx behind Galphay. Fireflow, again following their normal approach, and despite their alcohol fuelled aggression, behaved more deliberately. All harness was carefully checked and girths tightened before they mounted in unison having unfastened the head ropes attaching their beasts to the picket line. Carefully following the marketing plan and under the close direction of the Operations team, they moved off in strict formation. Mickley led, his imperious gesture lost in the night and they broke into a gentle trot as he moved away from them.

While the participants rode out, half whooping and yelling to encourage each other and build up their own courage, and half moving with an almost military precision, the unhelpful clouds once more obscured the moon. While this was distinctly awkward for Fang who had regained sufficient night vision to safely find the stairwell and started back down the crumbling, uneven, steps, it created far greater difficulties for the two sets of riders. The first, unnoticed tragedy that was to have dire effects on Coretec that night, occurred when the Resources Manager, a newly retired army officer and therefore capable of night navigation, while displaying all the aggression and panache instilled in him by the Parachute Regiment and so valued by Galphay, felt his saddle shift under him just as he thundered up on Galphay's left to suggest a change of course that would lead them in the general direction of the Fireflow base. Before he could try and rein in his wildly overexcited mount, he felt himself rotating and next moment was concussed as his head came rapidly into contact with the ground and acted as a form of brake on the animal. Before the pony stopped, being a sensible creature with a long exposure to the odd behaviour of occasional riders, the damage was well and truly done. The pony started to crop the grass and resisted the inclination to kick the nuisance that impeded its movement and made strange moaning noises that it did not like. As the Resources Manager's inverse pogoing went unnoticed, Galphay blindly charged on followed by the rest of his employees.

Despite their careful preparation, Fireflow unknowingly veered off course in the dark and started to swing to the right. While the sensible use of the Sales team as outriders and who had taken up position soon after the ride had started, saved the main body from several hazards such as ditches and soft ground, it did nothing to correct their rightward movement. Having regained the tower roof with a replacement torch, night vision scope and Alice and Sonya, Fang prepared to try and make sense of the teams progress so far.. All three stood listening and once or twice thought that they caught the sound of faint yells and screams on the night air but Alice feared that this was just wishful thinking. Fang rapidly discovered that the night scope was not as efficient as he had hoped but he finally picked up movement to the East. The Fireflow riders swam eerily into view and, obviously in formation, mysteriously disappeared back in the direction from which they had come.

Coretec were continuing to take casualties as a result of their bull headed approach. Four riders found themselves thrown into a patch of brambles that the ponies sensed as a loom in the dark and whose swerves of self- preservation were enough to unseat their incompetent riders. Shrieks rose as these unfortunates vanished into the thorny clutches of the vegetation that acted as a form of herbaceous barbed wire. Those riding furthest back in the Coretec horde saw their colleagues vanish screaming and reined in violently while the rest rode on, still solidly behind Galphay. Swearing, screams and curses rose from the brambles while several previously roosting pheasants exploded into the night sky. The would be rescuers attempted to dismount and still retain control of their ponies. One ended up joining her unfortunate colleagues in the depths of the brambles when her pony tired of her antics and bucked her off. The peculiar tone of her shrieks of horror and pain caused panic in the remaining ponies and two dragged their reins free of the despairing clutches of their dismounted riders and galloped away into the night. One of these hapless individuals sprinted off into the dark after his mount and soon a faint splash signalled the end of his chase. He returned soaked and shivering to assist in disengaging the last of the unseated from the brambles. The rescuers were in not much better condition than the rescued and, when the clouds once more cleared, the blood from myriad scratches shone black in the moonlight. After slapping the still shrieking and obviously hysterical erstwhile rescuer, they set about trying to remove thorns and stem the bleeding. They would take no further part in that night's action.

The first intimation of Fireflow's navigational error came to light when the Sales team sent back word that there was a set of buildings to their front. Immediately, they started to put their plans into action and it was only the rapid intervention of the previously despised office trainee that stopped a major mistake occurring. "They're ours!" He called urgently and, as various staff tried to hush him for contravening the clear instruction to keep noise to a minimum, started shouting. "Mr Mickley, they're ours. Mr Mickl..."

"His voice was cut off by the smothering gip of a large member of staff who lent across and covered his mouth. Mickley rode back to see what the fuss was and arrived just as the youth freed himself by biting the hand that covered his mouth and started bellowing in unison with the bitten. Mickley's horse reared at the sudden shouting and it was by more luck than judgement that he remained in the saddle. For once Mickley's veneer slipped.

"What the bloody hell are you clowns doing? He snarled, instantly quietening both. The office trainee gulped and spoke up.

"We've gone wrong Mr Mickley! Those buildings, they're ours! Can't you recognise them?" A terrible stillness fell over the group. No one had ever heard Mickley either swear or sound so ordinary before. Equally, no one could remember Mickley having a mistake he had made being pointed out to him. Mickley looked closely at the desperate youth then back at the buildings.

"Damn it!" He announced, instantly sounding like his normal self. He then amazed his staff. "Right, I've gone wrong, blasted dark! Any suggestions?" A faint murmur of incredulity died away as the Trainee spoke up again.

"It's simple really." He gulped "I mean, if you're used to it."

Mickley seemed to be on the same wavelength and grasped what he was being told. "So you're used to wandering around in the dark?"

"Oh yes, I grew up on a farm. We were often out and about at night." The Trainee refrained from explaining further, not sure how Mickley would regard poaching.

"You'd better lead then."

As Fireflow reorganised themselves to orientate in the right direction, Mickley could be heard enquiring of Marketing if they had bothered to carry out any research whatsoever. "I mean, seems quite straightforward to me, establishing if anyone of us was used to working in the dark. Hmm?" The hapless Marketing Director refrained from replying as the Trainee found himself stationed at the front of the column. On the way to the front he had nearly taken a nasty fall when a seemingly misguided pony blundered into his path, causing his mount to check.

"Sorry" Sweetness informed him out of the gloom. "Didn't see you there!" Secretly, she was furious that the Trainee had managed to get noticed favourably. They started off again with Mickley seemingly happy to follow the lead of the Trainee and Sales fanned out once more to screen the advance. In the dark, no one saw the poisonous looks that Sweetness directed towards the Trainee or witnessed the vicious whispered conversation amongst the marketers with regard to Mickley.

On top of the old peel tower, Alice had got hold of the night scope and, despite Fang's instructions to go easy on the batteries was still sweeping the darkened landscape for a sight of either team. Suddenly, she hissed. "They're back" as Fireflow emerged dimly on the screen before gradually disappearing into a fold of dead ground. Ignoring Sonya's pleas to let her have a look, Fang grabbed at the scope. A brief struggle ensued before he prised it from Alice's grasp.

"Come on," he ordered, we'll follow them and see how they get on." Alice disagreed.

"If we go out there and they bump into us, God knows what that bunch of thugs and perverts would do!" Sonya agreed vigorously, although she thought it might be fun to run into an individual team member in the dark. After a further brief discussion, Fang gave in with bad grace.

"Well, if you're too scared to follow them and do your job properly, we'll just stay here"

"Bloody right we will!" Alice informed him. Later, they wondered if they could have changed anything if they had been on the ground, but comforted themselves that it would have been very unlikely.

The hard thrusting riders of Coretec were still ignorant that their numbers were steadily decreasing as they became more strung out and the ponies tired. They were all to involved in trying to discern vague shapes as they loomed up in the dark and in the sudden changes of direction by the ponies around them as they avoided obstacles, to look about and try and count numbers. After a brief check at a stonewall where Galphay had surprised them all by bellowing "I'll give you buggers a lead" and kicking his pony at the obstacle. To the animal's amazement as well as those who could see anything, he sailed cleanly over before reining in to berate his reluctant followers. Showing slightly more sense, the Sales Director ordered a gap to be torn in the wall and they were soon through and breaking into a canter once more. Galphay avoided the loom of a forest on his left and pushed his pony on. The animal responded and indeed speeded up as the ground sloped gently down hill and sheep scattered at their approach. With increasing momentum, they thundered down hill. Just as one rider shouted to the dimly seen figure riding hard beside him

"Where the Hell are we going" and received the response

"Who knows!" They found the marsh.

The initial effect was that clods of mud and torn turves were thrown up by the hooves of the ponies and caused those at the rear to falter and slow in confusion. All the ponies slowed unbidden but those at the rear actually halted while the front runners blundered on. Finally, they all came to a halt as their mounts moved nervously, backing and whinnying. Those still on comparatively firm ground peered anxiously into the dark from which the sounds of mired ponies and riders emerged. "It's a bog" A horrified voice quavered followed by splashing noises. "We'll all drown!" Another shrieked. Galphay's angry bellows as he tried to restore order to the chaos, did not aid clear thinking.

"Should we help?" Enquired one of the drier members.

"I think they're having enough fun on their own." A colleague cautioned him. The ponies well into the marsh not unnaturally started to panic and soon had rid themselves of their encumbering riders as a series of yells and splashes told the listeners. Obeying their instincts, the ponies refused to move from what small tussocks they found to stand on and stood shivering but obdurate no matter how their former riders tried to drag them back in the direction of dry land. One by one, the soaked and mud encrusted splashed back to their waiting colleagues. The first effects of the ale had long worn off and they huddled together shivering and gazing out into the marsh as the scene was occasionally illuminated by the fitful moon. Undaunted, Galphay was still trying to encourage or, indeed, force, ponies into moving off their sanctuaries but they refused to move. At first the watchers were impressed by his determination but soon whispers regarding who had led them so effectively into the marsh developed. Galphay's cloak of impregnability was turning threadbare. It was to become positively torn by the end of the night.

Moving well under the guidance of the Management Trainee whose name no one could remember, he being the third such to join the company, the other two giving up their Year in Industry almost as soon as they realised what life in Fireflow was really like, the formation moved through the dark without drama. Even Sweetness had to admit to herself that the boy knew what he was doing. Their passage was noted by a hunting fox whose curiosity was piqued by the strange site of humans on horseback at night. It silently followed at a safe distance. A farmhouse was given a wide berth and, although a collie barked two or three times, there were no signs that anyone had been disturbed. The Sales team continued to warn of possible hazards and, as they moved on, were directed to move further ahead in teams of two to try and gain advance warning if any other riders were approaching. Up on the peel tower, their progress went unnoticed while Coretec were far from the true area of operations. All in all, the night appeared to lack any incident whatsoever to the watchers other than the strange manoeuvring of Fireflow earlier in the night. "You'd have thought they would have bumped into one another?" Wondered Fang but there was no sign of such an event having occurred. Sonya who had finally appropriated the night scope was using it to watch the rabbits in the field to the West when something flared. Her squeak of "What's that?" Mingled with Fang's shouts as a glow lit the near horizon.

"Alice! Alice! Isn't that where Coretec are camped?" Alice was startled out of her doze.

"What? What's happened?"

"There!" Fang pointed towards the brightening glow.

Fireflow had ridden in on Coretec's base screened by the Sales team and unerringly guided by the nameless Management Trainee. As soon as the first report came back that the building lay ahead, the Marketing plan had rolled smoothly into action. The first group as planned had kicked their ponies into a canter and ridden shouting and yelling into the fold yard to flush out any defenders who might have been lurking in the buildings, closely followed by a second wave of riders who had dismounted and passed their reins to designated horse holders before running into the buildings yelling and shouting. While they quickly searched the premises to make sure nothing living was present, the remainder sat on their ponies around Mickley acting as a rallying point while the Sales team rode further out to watch for the return of Coretec. In moments a glow was seen within the main barn and soon all the buildings were alight. The fire starters ran out and remounted and they moved swiftly back to the main body surrounded by the first wave. Uncharacteristically, Mickley lent forward in his saddle and spat in the direction of the now blazing old steading. "Ride!" He commanded and they turned and retraced their path towards their base at a steady canter. When he was sure that they had left, the fox bellied in to see if they had left any potential pickings but the smell of smoke and the noise as the roofs of the burning building collapsing sent him off into the safety of the near by trees.

Coretec eventually regrouped on the edge of the marsh as dawn provided enough light to finally persuade the ponies to leave their refuges. They splashed and splattered onto the drier ground and for the first time noticed the glow behind them. Galphay raved and swore but they paid remarkably little attention to him, remounting silently and following their own tracks through the grass. They found the tattered victims of the briar patch and the missing ponies drifted over to join them. Finally, as they crested the ridge to stare with incredulity and increasing rage at the smouldering remains of their erstwhile base, they found the concussed Resources Manager lying in the grass beside his pony which was quietly cropping the grass. He had finally freed his feet from the stirrups but seemed incapable of walking. Grimly, they righted his saddle and hoisted him onto the pony's back. A colleague on either side supported him as they moved slowly towards the ashes of their former rudimentary home. Galphay howled like a wolf and they edged away from him as he stood in his stirrups shaking his fist at the sky.

Chapter 9

With the coming of daylight, the glow from the former steading that had housed Coretec had turned into a thinning column of smoke. Fang coughed and spat. He had spent the remainder of the night, after driving furiously to the site to check that no one was injured or worse, in muttering darkly about irresponsible fools. He was still uneasy, as the fact that no one was standing around singed or scorched did not mean there had not been anyone trapped in the buildings. He circled the buildings again and again but, other than the glowing embers and the smoke blackened walls, there was nothing to be seen. "Christ, Alice, should I call the fire brigade? I mean" Alice had grown tired of this constant refrain.

"Look, they were meant to be all out on a training exercise and Galphay didn't seem the sort of man to accept anything short of death as an excuse to not participate. So.." She shrugged eloquently.

"Oh, for God's sake" Fang started again only to be interrupted by Sonya.

"Here they come now and they are all sort of there. I've counted them." Fang glared at her and then at the approaching band.

"What do you mean sort of…" He stopped when the import of Sonya's words were made clear by the sight of the Coretec contingent. Several looked as if they had been mauled by a particularly malevolent big cat, one was being supported in the saddle and was obviously concussed, at least half a dozen were covered in drying mud as were the majority of the ponies and Galphay appeared to be raving. Taken altogether, they were not a prepossessing sight. A relieved Fang moved into action. "Which clown left a fire burning?" He demanded, striding up to the unhappy band.

The situation was vastly different at Fireflow's encampment. Having groomed their ponies, the entire work force was celebrating the night's success. "Mickley raised his ale and toasted his triumphant followers. "Excellent work! Well planned, well executed! Splendid!" The majority cheered, the remainder being too foxed with drinking on empty stomachs to care. After a burst of spontaneous singing, one or two wondered where the promised food was following a successful exercise.

"Well, they won't be feeding over at Coretec will they!" The unknown Trainee gloated.

"Mind you, they'll be warm!" Remarked a programmer to universal groans. One or two stood and gazed out the holes in the wall for any sign of the promised food supplies coming and were soon rewarded by the site of Alice and Sonya approaching erratically over the field. Strangely, the fact that their vehicle was a horse drawn cart did not strike anyone as odd. Within eighteen hours it was as if they had moved back to a time before motor transport had been invented.

Things were rather more modern at the Coretec site where a doubly relieved Fang was expressing himself. "It's only by the grace of God that no one was killed. I would never have imagined that even you prats would have been so stupid as to leave an unattended fire burning amongst all that straw and hay." He paused momentarily for breath.

"Now, just you bloody listen…" Galphay objected only to find himself shouted down by Fang secure in the knowledge that they had signed a disclaimer regarding any injuries and that the training contract made the participants liable to pay for any damage that they caused during the course of their activities.

"Listen? Listen?" Bellowed Fang. "To what? Some damned stupid spurious excuse for your ineptitude? Dream on! First, you'd better see to the ponies, they look exhausted. Secondly, I'll be putting the cost of repairing this" He paused to vaguely wave a hand at the smouldering ruins "On your bill, and lastly" He added at the top of his voice as Galphay tried to interrupt him "Lastly, you'll be hungry by the time the next exercise is completed." A cross between a moan and a growl rose from the listeners. "You know the rules, failure means hunger. I'll have more ale delivered as obviously you drank the rest last night judging by your performance." He turned away then swung back. "You'll have the next exercise explained at noon." He stalked off back to his elderly pick up and drove away in a cloud of diesel fumes. Galphay regained his voice

"He can't speak to me like that .." He began to rage.

"Why not? Enquired a hungry accountant. "You can't claim we did anything right last night." Galphay was about to retaliate when the senior managers realised his position had been weakened and spoke up independently for the first time in years.

"Look" Operations stated to nods of agreement from his fellows. "Last night was a debacle. We got absolutely trashed. You lead, we followed. You got it wrong. You should learn from it." Galphay turned crimson with rage but the criticism showed no sign of abating despite his snarled threats.

"You little shit, I made this company.."

"And you nearly destroyed it last night." Galphay stepped forward, fists clenched but realised all his management staff were grouped together and not showing any signs of their normal fear in the face of his rage. Suddenly impotent, he stopped and glared at them.

"You run the company as you wish but you should stop making every decision yourself" Finance informed him. "You might find it better if you used the talent you've got and pay for but the choice is ultimately yours" Galphay started to laugh but suddenly realised that his employees were not laughing with him in their usual sycophantic fashion.

"I'm hungry, filthy and knackered and we didn't even find their camp." Announced a saleswoman. "Question is, what are you going to do about it?" Growls from the rest of the company backed the question menacingly. Galphay tried to regain control

"Question is, what are you going to do?" He responded.

"Wait for the embers to cool and then poke about trying to see if there is anything left that I brought. You're going to work out how to get those bastards back!" She swung a negligent arm at the management team. "Those losers should help you."

Her colleagues growled in agreement and Galphay and his senior employees found themselves huddled together and casting wary glances at the watching throng as they tried to work out what to do to rectify the situation.

Fireflow were contented. Well fed and having cleaned up somewhat following the nights activity, they had set guards according to the rota devised by Operations and were sleeping securely. The camp may not have been luxurious but they were too tired to care. Other than the sentries, only the senior managers were awake, holding a debrief on the night's activities and planning how they would respond to the next challenge. "The main thing," Planning announced, "is to remain organised but flexible. Be able to react quickly to whatever happens." Mickley raised an expressive eyebrow. "We spoke with that bloke from programming and got him to repeat everything and now we're thinking of what they might ask us to do and how to carry it out." Mickley yawned and Planning fell silent. Operations spoke up.

"We can take it as definite that Coretec will want to get their own back. They would anyway but as we're in the land of feud they're going to overreact!" Mickley smiled.

"I do hope so. Right, keep thinking, keep on top of things, and if you spot an opportunity to bring that shower down, let me know!" They all nodded in agreement and retired to sleep.

From Infant School, it had been obvious that Galphay did not accept criticism well. It was no different on this occasion but he realised that he would not be able to merely ignore it or persecute those who dared to regard him as less than faultless. Equally, through presenting a united front, his management team had stopped his favourite tactic of identifying a scapegoat to deflect blame elsewhere. He forced himself to listen to his managers in the hope that they might have something useful to contribute. It quickly became apparent that they did not and Galphay stood up suddenly.

"Keep thinking" He instructed them and strode off. They looked at each other and their angry fellow workers and started whispering to each other again. Galphay marched over to where the hapless Resources manager lay shielding his eyes from the glare of the daylight and nursing his aching head. Galphay kicked his feet. "You alive?"

"Just" Galphay waited but no more information was forthcoming.

"What are the best military tactics when you've taken a beating?"

"Counter attack" Came the laconic reply. Galphay suddenly grinned.

"They won't expect that, will they?"

"Never do" Came the response and Galphay strolled back to his managers.

Fang had overslept following the previous night's activities and it was not until well into the afternoon that he set off to inform the two teams of the next planned exercise. He decided that he would inform Coretec first as they would probably need more time to get organised judging by their first efforts. As he strolled towards the burnt out ruin that was the Coretec base, he was amazed to see them all in the saddle and milling around. "What the hell are they up to now?" He wondered and moved to intercept, breaking into a trot in order to head them off as they rode into the open field and shook themselves out into a loose formation. "Hey, hold on, I haven't told you what the next exercise is!" He shouted breaking into a run.

Galphay had used the intervening hours to rekindle belief in his bullish approach. First he had overcome the doubts of his management team, pointing out that he had consulted the only expert they had in this kind of operation and secondly by observing that they had come up with no ideas of their own in meeting the demands for revenge by their fellow workers. Finally, he had spoken to the rest. "Alright, I cocked up. Fair enough. Now, I want to do something about it. What do you lot want?" Carefully ignoring various shouts for proper leadership and selectively hearing only those calls for revenge, he gradually regained their grudging acceptance. Once he sensed that they were willing to listen to him, he started working on their emotions and pointed out how those Fireflow bastards had put one over on them all. "We were stupid," He announced. "We followed the rules and forgot something!" He took a deep breath. "There are no rules here, except to get our own back and win." His workforce nodded, some enthusiastically and he carried on working on their baser emotions. His cause was helped as the ale they had been replenished with was drunk "Now, I want to get those buggers back. Whose with me?" Ten minutes later, they were in the saddle and setting out for revenge. When Fang appeared suddenly in front of them, Galphay and the hotter heads were leading and were not in a mood to stop for anyone. "Move aside you bugger!" Galphay yelled and kicked his pony to speed up. The rest followed suit and Fang experienced the pleasure of being ridden over. For a few seconds, the world was a thunder of hooves, violent blows and fast moving bodies, before they were past leaving him bruised and winded in their wake.

Fang staggered to his feet. Bruised, battered and furious. "The bastard!" He wheezed and spat dust and pony hair. Had he bitten one of the bloody animals he wondered? He nearly sat down again involuntarily, but staggered and caught his balance again. Gradually, the feeling of dizziness faded and he spat and swore some more. Then, to the amazement of the watching figure that was the recuperating Resources Manager, Fang straightened and broke into a jog trot following the path taken by the Coretec riders.

"Hard bastard" the ex soldier muttered and unwisely shook his head in disbelief. When the pain had subsided to an acceptable level, the Resources Manager considered what would happen when Fang caught up with Galphay. He smiled nastily and carefully sat down again to await the outcome of Fang's chase.

Alice and Sonya were sitting on cushions on the steps at the back door, chatting about how the course seemed to be quickly pointing up the failings in both the participants and Fang as they sipped tea. "Ian's lovely" Alice sighed "But I thought he'd more drive, you know what I mean?" Sonya nodded.

"Yeah, he seems really sweet, but I never thought that he'd panic so much last night. It would have been their fault if they'd burnt themselves." Alice sipped more tea and absently patted the spaniel that regarded her with an air of disappointment.

"Look" She informed the dog "He flapped. I know he told them off but he still flapped. Maybe it won't work after all. I thought he was different." They fell into silence broken by the sound of running feet. Fang thundered round the corner and promptly rekindled all Alice's feelings.

"Saddle up!" He yelled before coughing and panting. "Go on, get moving, I'm going to crucify that bastard!" He straightened again and glared at them. They gazed back, taking in the hoof print on his chest, torn clothes, blackening eye and the crust of drying blood under his nose. "Move!" He bellowed. Alice nearly collapsed with suddenly rekindled lust, Sonya ran toward the stables and the spaniel farted evilly.

As the trio cantered in the direction that Fang had last seen Coretec heading, the girls tried to find out what had happened but Fang was too angry to explain properly and all they managed to determine was that Galphay was a bastard who would shortly wish he had never come within fifty miles of Fang. Far in their wake, the spaniel waddled in pursuit. He liked Fang who seldom bothered overmuch about cleanliness unlike the occasional housekeeper who had made his life hell. He could also sense violence in the air and had no intention of missing it so he toiled on. Behind them, for a moment it seemed as if the old tower leaned forward in anticipation.

Chapter 10

A crow, dawdling on the slight breeze that reflected off the slope of Bleakhope hill while it waited for something to become carrion, saw the Coretec riders moving in a herd like fashion far below. It's natural curiosity and instincts were aroused when it also spied the four moving shapes that were Fang, the girls and the dog, behaving like a hunting pack, fanning out behind the chase. In reality, Coretec's inability to navigate was, at the moment, protecting them from the wrath of Fang who had been unable to determine where the chase was headed and had ordered the girls to spread out to spot if in fact they were shedding riders to meet again at a prearranged rendezvous. Fang became both more confused and, if possible, angrier as the chase continued. In a similar fashion to the crow, he was following his own instincts and the veneer of civilisation had vanished under Coretec's hooves. He would not be satisfied until he gained revenge.

Coretec, themselves motivated by a strong desire for revenge on Fireflow and with their poor sense of direction made worse by drink, exhaustion and temper, were making good time heading for nowhere in particular. The rank and file were, at least temporarily, once more willing to follow Galphay's lead while the senior staff found they were too concerned on staying in the saddle to care about what direction they were taking. The fact that their leader rode into a pine forest served to allay any fears regarding where they were headed. Whatever they had had to contend with the previous night, a pine forest had not been one of them. Based on the principal that if they had they had not been here before probably illustrated that they were heading I the right direction, they rode on.

The FortyThird Glasgow Scout Troop had not, so far, particularly enjoyed their long awaited summer camp. The effect of Health and Safety and the fear of Litigation on a movement that had originally been created to produce independent young men who would fit easily into the military, had not increased the challenge or excitement for the participants. While their leader, an earnest, well intentioned young Minister and his two helpers, students who could not quite remember why they had volunteered, devoted their efforts to avoiding anything that could possibly lead to a situation where they might contravene the spirit and letter of the law, the boys devoted equal effort to subverting their good intentions. The result was that a form of undeclared mutiny hung in the air, orders were obeyed sullenly, warnings as to the dangers of such forbidden activities as cutting wood, damming the small burn to create a better swimming hole or night orienteering merely spurring the boys onto seeking more exciting alternatives. The previous night while the Minister pored in a worried fashion over the plethora of literature stipulating how to write up a risk assessment before taking the boys on a hike the next day, his helpers exhausted themselves in acting as sentries and heading off groups of boys who had been determined to carry out a night exercise. The result was that the adults were asleep despite themselves while the boys were too tired to be bothered to get up to anything. A small group were experimenting in creating slings with varying success, while several others had successfully raided the mess tent and were enjoying a quiet snack. The sudden apparition of Coretec at least provided a little excitement and a talking point.

Coretec had slowed slightly once they moved under the tree canopy. Galphay had unsurprisingly ridden where the trees were more mature and accordingly spaced further apart but the obvious thinning trees to his left had drawn him into the open and they all cantered into the field occupied by the scouts. It extended gently up hill, surrounded on three sides by trees that offered shelter from the weather and with a burn meandering through its centre. Altogether it was an idyllic campsite and one that the troop had been using for generations. Several boys emerged from tents to join some others who were already standing around to gaze at the Coretec riders who cantered past without slowing although several sets of eyes took in the neat rows of tents, fire pit and, most interestingly, Mess tent before the party rode back into the trees and were lost from view. If it had not been for the hoof marks that the scouts showed their disbelieving leader having woken him from his slumbers to tell him of the sudden spectacle, it was an almost dream like encounter.

Fang, meanwhile, was showing continuing signs of reverting to ancestral type. Having been checked in his pursuit on several occasions when Coretec had crossed hardened ground, he stopped and considered how best to catch up with them as it seemed they were showing considerable skill in using the land to make their progress hard to follow. The arrival of the spaniel who came rolling into view panting but otherwise going well, provided him with the solution. "Sleuth hound" He announced, pointing at the dog that seized the opportunity to sit down and catch its breath.

"What?" Queried Alice.

"The dog. He can trail the bastards, then we'll see how long they can keep ahead of us!" Alice and Sonya glanced at one another. This new Fang was vaguely unsettling in his determination. Sonya looked doubtfully at the panting animal that sat solidly in front of them. "He doesn't look up to it does he?" Fang grinned

"Only one way to find out!" If the spaniel was surprised to find himself trotting in front Fang to shouts of "Hi Lost!" he did not show it, choosing instead to follow the obvious scent trail of hot horses and stale alcohol that filled his nostrils.

Coretec, after half an hour in the forest, were beginning to panic. It was obvious to all that Galphay had lost his bearings and, as the rest had been blindly following him, they had no better idea them selves. The pine forest had become a trap that they seemed unable to escape. The trees, to some, assumed a menacing aspect that they found deeply unsettling. As they continued to trot in a haphazard fashion, the deadening effect of the drifts of pine needles on the sound of the ponies' hooves also served to increase their sense of foreboding. One accountant uttered a scream when a howl carried through the woods. As one, they stopped and huddled closer together gazing wide eyed in the direction the sound had seemed to come from.

The spaniel gazed reproachfully up at Fang whose pony had accidentally kicked it when it had checked momentarily and the beast had been unable to avoid it. Fang encouraged the spaniel loudly. "Good dog! Hi Lost! Work the bastards!!" Muttering to itself, the spaniel which had enjoyed making a fuss once it had realised it had not really been hurt, set off once more. This time, it had no intention of being trodden on, and it increased its speed accordingly. Assuming that the increased speed meant that the dog had now hit on a hot scent, Fang uttered a whoop of excitement that Alice and Sonya, caught up in the moment despite themselves, mirrored with enthusiasm. The spaniel, despite his growing exhaustion, howled in answer. The effect on Coretec, or more particularly their ponies, of the sudden noise was startling. Having picked up the increasing nervousness of their riders, the ponies were predisposed to panic. The first howl had stirred dark, atavistic memories and the second chorus had convinced them they were being lined up as part of the food chain by a pack of rapidly closing wolves. To a beast, they screamed in panic, rearing and bucking frantically and kicking out at one another in a frenzy as their riders tried to restrain them or, in several cases, encouraged them in trying to bolt from the oncoming danger.

Fang and his 'hot trod' rode into a clearing to find it filled with panicking ponies with swearing struggling riders clinging desperately to their reins, while several fallen riders were crawling among the pine needles pathetically trying to dodge their former mounts who were wildly galloping in circles. Despite himself, Fang burst into laughter at the sight. Finally, he caught himself and demanded of the shamefaced Coretec "What in God's name are you up to?"

A muttered chorus of "Lost again! Wolves! Ponies panicked!" Left him slightly confused but still amused. Grasping at the essential fact that they were lost once more, reminded him that he had been pursuing them for a reason.

"We'll show you how to get back to your base. Now, before we do, can anyone explain why you thought it was acceptable to ride over me today? Or is it just that you're total buffoons without the common sense to think of consequences?" Galphay felt it necessary to try and intervene in the growing tirade.

"Only a bloody fool runs in front of ponies! You deserved everything you got!" Fang's temper reappeared with a vengeance.

"You stupid little man" His voice dripped scorn. "If you weren't so pathetic I'd end this whole training exercise now. Obviously you're deaf as well as terminally bloody thick If you didn't hear me shouting or see me running towards you waving my arms, you prat, no wonder you're permanently lost!" Galphay, infuriated, jumped off his horse and strode towards Fang who dismounted and stood with a sneer on his face.

"I'll give you bloody thick!" Galphay yelled and took a swing at Fang.

Thirty seconds later, Fang glared around him at the encircling throng. "Does anyone else want to try anything or shall we just get you back to base?" The only response was a groan from Galphay who was too preoccupied with his badly bruised groin to care about his other injuries. Fang bent and helped him up by his ponytail. The crowd winced and the spaniel broke wind in approval. "You!" He commanded an accountant. "Help him walk, he won't want to ride for a while. The rest of you, follow me." Galphay swore gently and monotonously while the accountant held an arm gingerly. "For Christ's sake!" Fang made an obvious effort to master his temper. "Sonya, can you wait and make sure the idiots find their way back while Alice and I guide this bunch?" Sonya agreed and watched Fang climb into his saddle and move off closely followed by Alice and the plainly pleased if exhausted spaniel. The bulk of Coretec followed at what seemed a safe distance talking earnestly to one another. The senior managers had stayed with their fallen leader, not merely from long ingrained fear and loathing but also to enjoy his discomfort and the fact that they did not know what to do without him.

In the event, having finally got a still uncomfortable Galphay and his chastened followers back to the seemingly under populated encampment, Sonya found that neither Fang not Alice there, nor were they at Bleakhope when she rode back there. In the event, Alice had found the new, masterful Fang a considerable turn on and the sight of him beating the larger Galphay with nonchalant ease had left her almost squirming with ill concealed lust. As soon as she had managed to drag him away from Coretec who he had been lecturing hard on navigation for the whole of the return journey, she gave way to her feelings. She had stopped her pony, dismounted hurriedly and dragged Fang off his, before positively tearing her clothes off. To Fang's surprised delight, he had spent the rest of the afternoon making passionate love while their ponies grazed quietly nearby and the spaniel, while pretending to sleep, kept a lecherous watch on their antics. Tired but happy, they did not return until dusk was falling.

The Coretec rank and file had watched Fang's efficiently vicious beating of Galphay with interest and considerable surprise. They had been quiet as they followed the lecturing Fang back to their base, not choosing to run the risk of annoying him. In the event, they also listened to his advice with interest as he explained how to avoid getting lost and actually reach a planned destination in good order. He had then taken the opportunity to try and enlighten them as to how the reivers had operated and they had taken on board his strictures on seizing the main chance with alacrity. It was perhaps unfortunate that they had passed the scout camp shortly after Fang had informed them that if the reivers had required something to ensure their existence they took it. After sitting around for several minutes once Fang and Alice had hurried away, discussing Galphay's stupidity and unfitness for leadership, the talk had turned to food or rather the lack of it. Wear, well aware of his unpopularity with his fellow workers, pointed out that a little effort would provide a swift solution.

"What the hell are you on about?" demanded one of the sales team.

"Food!" Wear replied. "Come on, you all saw that camp with a few scouts wandering around. I can't have been the only one to notice their mess tent! Why don't we just ride over and make sure we have something to eat tonight." There were several nods of agreement and support.

"Grab some tents as well! Suggested a previously shy and retiring programmer. They looked at her and she reddened but stuck to her view. "It'll be cold tonight, we need shelter as well as food due to that idiot Galphay!" The others could only agree with this statement.

Finally showing some cunning, Coretec separated into good and indifferent riders, with the latter being left to improve defences in the area surrounding the former buildings. The Resources manager had sufficiently recovered to start making useful suggestions as to the sighting of pits and other traps around the place and they set to with a will as their colleagues rode out on the first true raid of the Training week. None seemed to care that this was not part of the official programme indeed, its very illegality served to improve their whole approach. Rather than bump into their returning leader and his loyal servants, they took a wide sweep over the fields, keeping to dead ground as much as possible before entering the wood leading their ponies on foot to reduce the possibility of noise.

The first the Forty Third Glasgow Scouts knew of the attack was when they felt the ground tremble slightly and a faint drumming grew louder. "Now boys, I will just have a look outside," The Reverend McLeod announced before Coretec erupted into the camp. The minister stepped out of the tent only to reel back from a kick administered by a passing rider, to fall at their feet. The boys looked at his prostrate figure, then rushed to get outside, closely followed by the two student helpers. Calling upon the Almighty, the minister staggered to his feet and exited the tent once more. The scouts, following the lead of the two students who seemed to have forgotten their divinity studies, were endeavouring to bring down any rider they could by sheer weight of numbers. The unknown thugs seemed sadly to be having the best of it, easily avoiding the attempts to drag them off their mounts. Noticing several riders had dismounted at the mess tent, McLeod set off at a run towards them, pausing only to yell at a small scout who had produced a strictly illegal sheath knife and was trying to hamstring any pony he felt he could reach. "No, Donald, and I want that knife as soon as this is sorted!"

The riders grabbing all the food they could, were somewhat surprised when a slightly built young man with a rapidly developing black eye waded into them throwing punches and calling on the Lord to smite the ungodly in a Hebridean accent. Showing a remarkable lack of interest in self defence, McLeod concentrated on trying to beat off the mob from his charges' food, throwing punches with abandon and soaking up retaliation without flinching. The students, realising that their Leader and Minister was battling alone, called on the scouts to rally and support.

"Get thae bastards!" And

"Pit the boot in and look tae the Minister!" rang out. The Forty Third, showing the true scouting spirit, did their best to comply and, wielding whatever weapon they could find from tables to tent poles, fought towards the melee at the former mess tent. By now, still calling on his Lord for strength, the Church Militant, had been reduced to hugging as many tins of food as he could to his chest as Coretec tried to make a clean sweep of the supplies. The arrival of the scouts ended that particular incident and the boys gazed in awe at the battered figure of McLeod. As his assailants hurriedly remounted and rode away, he remembered Health and Safety

"Now, Donald, pass me the knife and we will not mention it again." Donald complied thinking the Minister would probably make better use of a blade than he could, but disappointingly McLeod merely staggered to his feet and wrapped the knife in some torn cardboard he picked up. Bruised, bloodied but unbowed, McLeod counted heads anxiously before, reassured, he looked around at the wrecked camp. "Oh Dear" he announced. "This will take some time to mend." Ignoring the clamour for bloody revenge from his troop, he contemplated the wreckage. "Vandals" he announced and went to wash the blood from his face.

The Coretec riders rode triumphantly back to their base, loaded with booty in the form of food and several tents. Their arrival was greeted with cheers from their colleagues who had been preparing defences and scowls from senior management who took their cue from Galphay. "What the hell have you been doing?" He demanded.

"Sorting things out, at least we've food and shelter despite you!" Wear unwisely informed him. Soon a party atmosphere pervaded the Coretec ranks as a meal was hastily prepared, tents put up and ale consumed. Despite himself, Galphay gave a grim smile of approval. At last they were showing some spirit though that little bastard Wear could kiss any hopes of a career good bye once they returned to London.

From some nearby gorse bushes, several scouts watched with looks of malevolence. They had easily trailed Coretec back to their base, their departure unnoticed by the Students or the reverend McLeod who were all too bruised and battered to pay much attention. "Ah'll get one o' yon bastards" The newly knifeless smallest scout whispered, loading his sling with a pebble and starting to whirl it. The now recovered Resources manager strolled between two tents to check the boundary defences and the pebble bounced off his skull unnoticed by anyone else. He subsided with a muffled curse. The scouts crawled off silently through the gorse and vanished to tell their colleagues of the success of their reconnaissance. Coretec carried the re-concussed Resources manager into a tent deciding that he was suffering from a relapse, unaware they were now at feud with the Forty Third Glasgow Scouts as well as Fireflow and that they had lost their natural war leader.

Chapter 11

The next day dawned with a cold breeze and smirring rain. Coretec slept late, for once well fed and with shelter from the elements. Fireflow had used the evening to continue making their steading more acceptable and had slept well as a result. Fang woke to find Alice still feeling amorous and they fell asleep again shortly thereafter. Sonya and the spaniel were both exhausted from the previous day's activities and slept deeply. The scouts had spent the night in overcrowded tents and suffering from only having baked beans left to eat following the depredations of Coretec and had slept little as a result. The Reverend McLeod had not slept at all, having spent the night inwardly debating if his beliefs had been contravened by the use of violence in defending his charges, while his bruises ached. Full light found the scouts standing in shivering groups or picking once more at the debris at the former site of the mess tent in a pathetic search for food. When they were called together for a roll call, it quickly became obvious several were missing. The minister started to wring his hands but stopped when he realised he was aggravating his bruised knuckles. Somehow he controlled his anger and relief when Donald and the rest reappeared. "Where have you been?" He enquired. Mutely they produced several dead rabbits and a pheasant. The troop regarded the minister with interest as he visibly wrestled with his conscience. Finally, he overcame his scruples. "Well, it's a start. Does anyone know how to er, clean this food?" Donald spoke up.

"Gie us ma knife and ah'll soon hae them ready!"

McLeod lost his appetite as he guarded Donald from the dangers of his knife and dressed the animals himself.

Following a leisurely breakfast, Fang agreed that it was time to move onto the next training exercise. "Hopefully, they will all have learnt enough by now to actually get from place to place without getting lost." Sonya announced.

"You'd like to think so, I mean they can all sort of ride now can't they?"

Alice was also feeling positive. "We'll see, but it's not fair to that Fireflow bunch just because Coretec are incompetent!" Fang scowled at the thought of Coretec and particularly Galphay but the entrance of the spaniel seeking a late breakfast distracted him and soon they hurried from the pungent smelling room. "We might as well get going!" Alice announced.

"Well, we need to tell them how they are getting on so far" Sonya announced firmly. Fang sighed.

"We'll get them organised for the next part of training and then I'll call a Warden's court and tell them how they're doing with the other lot listening. Should keep them busy and increase the competition!" The girls looked dubious.

"It will certainly get them upset, think how Galphay will react," Alice cautioned.

"Exactly!" Fang responded and refused to debate the issue any further. The spaniel watched them go and went to lie down again. It knew it would need all its energy later.

Fireflow were obviously restless and keen to get on with the next training exercise when the trio arrived on pony back to inform them what was to happen next. "You may have noticed that you have some cattle living near you!" Fang announced. "They are there for a reason. The reivers main activity was cattle rustling. Now, each day you will be awarded extra food if your cattle numbers have increased. It will not surprise you to hear that your opponents at present have an equal number of cattle. They will be getting the same information as you. Obviously then, the team that lifts the most, to quote the reivers, wins." He paused while Fireflow looked back at where the cattle grazed unconcerned and then back at Fang. "The exercise starts at dusk so no jumping the gun but after that any time is good. Now, I'm going to hold a warden's court at noon when both sides get told how they are getting on and to cover any minor administrative details." He then spent some time explaining that on a Warden's day, a truce was completely observed and even feuds suspended from sunrise to sunset. Mickley smiled.

"We quite understand. Thank you and see you at noon."

When they reached the Coretec encampment, they were surprised to find several tents and some of the Coretec contingent eating. After exchanging quizzical glances, Fang spurred forward and launched into his speech. He resisted asking where the tents and food had come from until Coretec reacted badly at the thought of a Warden's day where their failings would obviously be aired in front of their rivals. "Instead of shouting at me, can anyone explain where the tents and food came from?" He demanded. Galphay spat eloquently. "Very well, we'll discuss it further at noon. Now remember, the truce lasts until sunset. Clear?" He wisely decided that a muttered chorus of "Fuck off!" signalled agreement and rode off followed by the girls. "Where the hell have they found the tents and food?" Fang wondered. The girls had no answer and he reined in to look back at the Coretec camp. Rather unnervingly, they were standing together just watching Fang and the girls.

"They certainly seem to be forming stronger bonds!" Sonya remarked.

"Stupid bastards" Fang responded and kicked his mount into motion.

Oddly, Fang was unsurprised when Alice and Sonya returned from a trip to the village shop with news that a vicious bunch of hooligans had smashed up a scout camp. "It must be that lot who come from Glasgow each year. "Fang mused.

"Who? The hooligans?" Sonya enquired.

"No, for God's sake, the poor bloody scouts. What the hell were they playing at?"

Alice sighed. "Surviving I suppose. I mean they must be hungry by now!"

"Alice, they've been out assaulting children and stealing their food. That's hardly justifiable is it?" Alice shrugged. "Well, we've been encouraging them to think independently and to remember that the end justifies the means. So long as no one connects them with us!" Fang stared at her.

"They're not are they?" She shook her head.

"Nope, just blaming the yob culture etcetera." Fang considered silently for a moment or two.

"I'd better warn them as to what is unacceptable although Coretec did seem a little, well, feral earlier didn't they?"

Noon saw Coretec and Fireflow bristling at each other with more than a hint of latent violence that Alice and Sonya found frankly terrifying. If Fang felt the slightest hint of unease, he refused to show it as he rode between the two factions. In fact, he was rather surprised to find that Coretec had managed to reach the rendezvous at the appointed time. Fang sat on his pony and waited for the trading of mutual insults to die down, but when they showed no sign of abating, he held up an imperious hand for silence. A last cry of "Fire starting bastards" faded away and Fang smiled unpleasantly. "Ladies and Gentlemen," He announced " Thank you for meeting here today. As I explained earlier, the Warden's court is an opportunity to judge recent events and administer judgement. Today I will tell you how you are getting on with regard to the training, In future, if either side feels that something unfair has been done by the other side, bring it here and it will be sorted." He waited a moment before speaking over the growing noise from either side. "One thing you need to remember, in the past, all judgements depended on oath giving. If the reivers swore they had not done something then they were judged innocent. Equally, they could be sworn against and the warden totted up the oaths on either side and gave weight depending on who swore. Clear?" General snarls and muttering made it clear they had all heard his words even if they did not accept them. "Right, onto how things have gone so far."

Out of the corner of his eye, Fang noticed that Alice and Sonya were edging clear of the two groups who were now pressing inwards. "Back, damn you!" Fang unknowingly quoted a former warden whose approach had been unappreciated by those he had been judging. "May I remind you that this is a training scheme?" He enquired as the two parties started to snarl insults at each other again. It was apparent that if he did not regain control then violence was likely to start and he would be caught in the middle. Strangely this appeal to more modern thought reduced the tension as one or two saw the absurdity of their behaviour and laughed aloud. "Now, move back and you can all hear what I have to say." He whistled silently with relief and glanced back to make sure that Alice and Sonya were at a safe distance. Realising that he was sweating with the tension, Fang decided to try and lower the temperature before making any judgement or raising issues such as possible arson or assaulting children for food and shelter.

"Now, I think that you will find that the course will become more exciting and, indeed satisfying from now on." He announced.

"Wouldn't be hard" carried clearly and Fang pretended to laugh.

"No, really, I think you will enjoy protecting and lifting cattle! They have a mind of their own which makes things interesting and you can make full use of your ingenuity in trying to do better than the other side." A growing chorus of "Wankers!" and "Tossers!" Rolled over Fang's head and his pony cavorted as the growing tension made it nervous in turn.

The Forty Third Glasgow Scouts had leopard crawled as close as they could to the warden's meet but the open nature of the ground and short cropped grass had stopped them getting near enough to hear what was going on. The occasional shout could be heard but they concentrated on trying to identify their assailants. "Ah ken that yin! Ye can see the bruises whaur the minister stuck the heid on him!"

"Aye, ye can, big nosed bastard"

"Eh? The minister disnae!"

"No the minister, him"

"Oh, aye, right enough." They stared hard and gradually spotted more of their enemies. At the same time, it became apparent that their enemies had foes of their own and quite what Fang was trying to do eluded them.

"Whit's that yin up tae?"

"Ah dinnae ken but it looks awfae risky!" It seemed that Fang agreed with the hidden watchers as he suddenly kicked his pony out of the throng before wheeling to face them again.

Fang had found the last few minutes rather startling. For a few moments he had thought that he has successfully calmed the situation by introducing the idea of the next exercise. However, the reaction from both Coretec and Fireflow had stunned him. Faces contorted with mutual hatred and threats were freely hurled, as both sides informed the other what they intended to do. His efforts to restore calmness had failed utterly and had only seemed to focus the rage and hatred on himself. Despite his normal willingness to fight anyone regardless of their size, Fang was well aware that he could not hope to take on this angry mob. As they surged around him, he had managed to win free due to elbowing one particularly pressing individual and forcing his pony through the gap made when his victim had wrenched his own mount aside. Once out of the throng, Fang turned and yelled at what he still naively thought of as trainees. "What in God's name are you playing at?" His angry bellow somehow attracted their attention and broke the escalating mood of febrile excitement. "Get into your groups and listen to me!" To Alice's amazement, they did as commanded and pulled apart. "For the last time, this is training!" Fang informed them loudly. "Both sides are obviously strengthening their team spirit but" He stopped to glare the first would be protester into silence. "But, this seems to be going too far. If I hear of any more accidental fires " Fireflow started to talk loudly and Fang resorted to shouting again "Or assaults on innocent children" This time Coretec added their voices to the attempt to drown out the accusations. The scouts managed to hear the bellowed comment on assaults on innocent children.

"Innocent? Wha's innocent?" Donald enquired.

"The minister!"

"Whit are they daen noo?"

Coretec and Fireflow were pulling apart in a flurry of shaken fists, raised fingers and bawled insults. Fang sat his pony, statue like, as the two sides separated. A sense of impending disaster made him inwardly quail but he resolutely tried to project the idea that he was both aloof and in control. Sadly he realised it was more that neither side really noticed him or felt he was worthy of attention while there was a foe to be threatened. As Coretec and Fireflow kicked their mounts into a canter and departed the scene, Alice and Sonya rejoined Fang both looking rather shocked and scared. "What is happening Ian?" Alice appealed.

"I have a horrible feeling they are really taking it all too seriously. God knows where it will end" Fang responded prophetically.

The scouts, still concealed in the long grass, let the trio ride through their midst without alerting them to their presence. Once Fang and the girls were well away, they sat up. "So," an older boy announced "They bastards hate yon others!"

"Aye" the rest agreed.

"Right, we need tae find where yon others bide and we'll mak them allies!" They all growled in assent before leopard crawling back to the waiting forest.

Chapter 12

The confrontation with the loathed Mickley and his Fireflow seemed to have totally rekindled Galphay's enthusiasm and self belief. As they cantered back to their base, Coretec gradually realised that he had once more assumed what he saw as his rightful place and was laying down the action that he proposed to take to regain the upper hand over his hated rival. The majority of Coretec found this strangely comforting, particularly as they now knew that they could temper his wilder actions if they stood up to him in a group and presented alternatives with sufficient force. In the mean time, they were content to let Galphay rant and plot while they rode. It still had not sunk in how great a loss the second injury to the Resources manager was, and overall Coretec were at their most confident since the training course had begun.

Fireflow had moved swiftly back to their base having ensured that the Sales force acted as a screen to their rear in case Coretec decided to break the day long truce. Once back, Mickley quickly called a meeting with his senior staff to decide on their plans. "Two objectives!" Mickley announced. "Lift their beasts and look after our own. Suggestions?" Marketing naturally felt the need to offer up a plan and the usual dickering began over the best use of resources. They had just decided that the best method would be to split their force in two, with half guarding the cattle and the rest riding out to hopefully lift Coretec's, when the office trainee strolled over and hovered diffidently on the edge of the group. Ignoring the angry glances from Marketing and Operations who felt that he should leave planning to those who understood it, the trainee waited until he caught the eye of Mickley, who gestured him over.

"Well, my boy?" Mickley was at his most revoltingly avuncular but the trainee seemed unaware that this was normally a sign of danger. The senior managers moved slightly away from him to avoid being caught up in the anticipated row.

"I've been thinking." The trainee announced.

"Remarkable!" Mickley announced. The trainee grinned, oblivious to the sarcasm.

"We don't want to play into their hands do we? No." He agreed with himself. "They are sure to guard their cattle with a fair number of their people and send out the rest to try and get ours.."

"Well, obviously" Marketing started only to be interrupted.

"Exactly! What we need is to be in a position where we can apply overwhelming force to lifting their beasts. Only way we can do that is to have more riders out." Operations waved at Marketing to quiten the next interruption. "Only way we can do that, is leave only a few guards with our cattle, lead some of their guards away and pile in on what remains!" Mickley looked up at the trainee.

"How do you propose, we, ah, free up people to overwhelm that shower?"

The trainee grinned. "Well, they're so stupid that they'll keep their cattle close to their base. We move ours and hide them with just a few people left to stop them straying, then we take a sweep to get in behind them, let them see a few to chase and then go in. No problem!" Mickley nodded slowly.

"Very well. You're in charge of the night's operations. Tell this lot what you want and they'll make it happen."

With Coretec once more being driven hard by Galphay, they showed remarkable efficiency in getting organised ready to start as soon as the sun set. "Bloody simple!" Galphay announced. "Half stay to guard our cattle, the useless bastards, the rest of us ride over and grab theirs. Questions?" They looked at each other then back at Galphay. One or two felt that it was perhaps a little straightforward but felt unable to express their concerns, knowing that the slightest hesitation would draw down Galphay's rage. "Right, we get something to eat, check the ponies, then pull all the cattle together by the steading. Or what remains of it! " He observed bitterly. Grateful to the scouts for their unwilling contribution to their well being, they soon organised a meal. The cattle were remarkably amenable with regard to being driven together and moved into the hollow of ground near the remains of the steading. "Right, three or four ride round as sentries, the rest can build up a fire to illuminate the area!" The Resources manager nursing his by now perpetual head ache, muttered in disagreement but went unheard as he lay alone in a tent. With their usual bustle and haste, Coretec were rapidly organised, "Now, can anyone remember what that snivelling little git said about navigation?" Galphay enquired in his usual reasonable tones. They all understood that he was referring to Fang and kept quiet. Cursing, Galphay turned away for a moment then swung back. "Right, get yourselves sorted and we'll make a start. I want to catch those bastards with their pants down." Before full dark, Coretec's raiding party rode out.

The first runner returned panting to the scout camp. "They bastards are on the move!"

"Whit wa'?"

"Doon by the watter "

"Right, Jamesie, tak Snort and lead them aff." The student looked across at his friend. "How's himsel'?" The other pondered.

"A bit deep in thought, off in a bit of a ponder."

"Aye, weel, we'll tak care o' things!" The next returning scout brought news of Fireflow.

"They're awa' ower the moss in'na sweep, ye ken!"

"Right, get awa tae they're camp and tell yon guards whit's comin' they're way. Mind, Snot may lead them aff!" The scouts ran to and fro, bringing information and vanishing to all parts with commands and warnings. It would not be from lack of effort that they would not play a part in the night's activities or its outcome. Ignorant of the scheming and activity, the Reverend McLeod contemplated the meaning of infinity and man's place in it as he gazed at the stars.

Unknowing, Coretec rode through an invisible web of small watchers as the scouts trailed their every move and tried to get Jamesie and Snot in a position to intercept them. Their task was made harder by the fact that Coretec remained poor navigators in addition to their trying to follow what Galphay believed was a circuitous route. The combination added miles to the distance covered and not only the scouts but also the ponies were beginning to feel the pace. At last, the scouts correctly divined the direction that Galphay was taking and, with a final sprint got Snot in position. "Dinnae fuck up!" He was sternly warned, then Jamesie faded into the shadow of a bush. Galphay reined to a savage halt that nearly led to multiple injuries as his followers desperately tried to avoid his suddenly stationary figure.

"For Christ's sake!" He bellowed.

"I'm terribly sorry, I did not mean to startle you." An impeccably accented child's voice informed him.

"Look, son, you could have got hurt. Now bugger off home!" The voice trembled with emotion as it responded to Galphay's instructions.

"Well, I would, sir, but I got lost running away from some people driving cattle over there."

"Over where?" Galphay let his sudden excitement show in his voice.

"If you follow me, I can show you..."

"Right, lead on and you'd better be bloody right."

"Absolutely!"

"Come on!" Galphay ordered his followers, "Now we've got them!"

Jamesie followed discretely, ready to try and help Snot if his ruse was discovered. That Snot, he chuckled as he ran, yon snotty accent sounded like nothing he'd ever heard. What was even better, yon tosser had believed in it, just like yon students had said. "Fucking brilliant" He chortled and trotted on, a faithful shadow.

Back at the Coretec camp, the watch fire blazed mightily and at first, the guards had been delighted in its warmth and light. As the night wore on, one or two realised that they could see no further than the light it cast, having ruined their night vision with its blaze. The rest seemed oblivious to this drawback and happily piled on more wood and straw as soon as it started to die down. Spirits rose when the merits of mulled ale were discovered, with a poker being heated in the flames then plunged into tankards to warm the contents. One or two even started to sing and the thought of not having to trail across the darkened landscape behind Galphay completed the general sense of well being felt by the majority. It came as a considerable shock when they heard the sound of rapid hoof beats approaching. The initial thought was that Galphay was returning, rapidly followed by the realisation that a raid was driving in on them. They scrambled onto their ponies as best they could and, shouting at the sentries to hold the cattle rode headlong out to meet the threat. It was not until several hard riding figures erupted whooping out of the dark and into the firelight that they could clearly see what was happening and, with yells of their own, they took off after them as they turned and vanished once more into the night.

Out on the edge of the darkness, Mickley curled a lip like a ferret that has just been informed of the existence of mexymitosis and what it meant. He could clearly see the milling, lowing cattle, who did not like being rudely awakened, were guarded by only four riders. "Right chaps, take them. Oh, and the incompetents with them. They might ransom, don't you think?" With a menacing lack of show, Fireflow emerged from out of the dark like a nightmare. The remaining Coretec riders were not lacking in courage or else were motivated by fear of Galphay's response if they lost their cattle. In any event, they endeavoured to take the fight to the enemy. A brief, if savage, melee broke out before they were unhorsed and subdued. While the guards were being despatched, several of the Fireflow riders ignored the brawl and quietly walked their ponies around the cattle to keep them bunched. As soon as the order came to move, they started to gently drive the cattle, building up to a steady canter as more riders joined them to hedge in the beasts so they could only go forwards. The whole mass, including the former guards now tied to their ponies, set off back towards Fireflow's base.

Coretec had been following Snot on what seemed a convoluted trail for some time when, as they passed through a small wood, he vanished. It took several moments to realise that their guide had disappeared and considerably longer to search the wood unavailingly for any sign of him. Further delay occurred when Galphay tried to catch the owner of the voice that yelled "Stupid wankers!" out of the dark. Eventually, they decided that there was nothing further to be gained and, after a bitter diatribe from Galphay that led several to openly question his sanity, they rode off. Snot gave it several minutes before climbing down from the tree in which he had been roosting and, hooting mournfully like an owl, went in search of Jamesie. Congratulating each other and sniggering over what they had achieved, they set off back to the camp.

In the event, the warning conveyed to Fireflow's cattle watchers by the scouts, had been as unnecessary as moving the beasts into the shelter of a wood. Coretec failed to appear before the sound of drumming hooves signalled the return of the main body together with their prizes and hostages. Soon, they were all toasting the suddenly enlarged herd while the two groups of Galloways grew acquainted with each other. Coretec were not so happy. The realisation that they had been falsely guided was quickly followed by the knowledge that they were bound to have been tricked further. A wild sense of loss as they realised that their cattle would be gone together with the thought of yet another hungry day as the scouts' contribution was virtually eaten, led to a headlong gallop back to their camp. It was even worse than they had imagined. Not only had all the cattle gone, but so had the sentries. The glow from the embers of the fire as they were stirred by the night breeze, somehow added to the sense of overwhelming defeat. When the Resources manager crawled from his tent to inform them of what had happened, they gazed in horror at the messenger while Galphay's face worked uncontrollably. A furious murmur of "No food" ran through the ranks only to be interrupted by Galphay.

"He just said increase your number of cattle?" He enquired furiously.

"Yeh, so what?" Galphay lent forward and spat on the ground.

"So, there are cattle on that farm we passed earlier. We'll lift them!" Coretec experienced a primal thrill at the thought.

"Are there enough?"

If not, we visit the next farm until there are!" Galphay felt a warm surge of pleasure despite the failure of the night so far. Despite everything, they were still with him. Without another word, he led off, followed by his staff.

The Reverend McLeod was unhappy. He had suddenly realised that the scouts were not in the camp and there was no indication of where they had gone. His pleasant reverie was shattered by nightmare visions of drowned scouts, scouts falling out tress, scouts wandering lost in forests until they starved, raced through his mind's eye. Stopping only for a brief prayer and to admonish God for letting his guard slip, he set off to look for his charges. The scouts had regrouped with military precision at the appointed rendezvous laid down by the students, and were listening to Snot explain how he had crawled into some bushes then up a tree to leave Coretec bewildered. Their laughter when Jamesie recounted the reaction of Coretec to his shouted insult, sent them into hysterics. It was the noise of merriment that led the minister to find them and he was rapidly mollified by the students. "Aye, well, you were contemplating and needed some quiet, and the lads have been good all week, so we took them for a night stroll tae listen for owls. Then we've been telling stories for entertainment. Eh, lads?"

"Oh, aye, stories were awfie guid so they were!" McLeod smiled, touched that they had been thinking of him.

"Well, I shouldn't have doubted you, but you know you should have written a plan and let me know."

"Aye, well, it was spontaneous and meant tae give you some peace tae think."

"Well, well, we'll say nothing more of it. Now, have any of you heard of the headless horseman ?" The scouts sniggered quietly and admitted they had not. McLeod loved to tell stories and they knew he would forget to enquire anymore about their night stroll. In the event, the story of the headless horseman proved unforgettable as, just at the denouement, galloping hooves were heard drumming through the night.

The same sound had awakened Hungry Knowe farm, that and the lowing of cattle and the hysterical barking of the sheep dog. "What the hell is going on?" Enquired Hungry Knowe of his wife.

"Horse racing?" She replied sleepily.

"More like cattle racing" He remarked before the import of his words sank in. "My beasts!" He yelled leaping out of bed and rushing for the door. His wife heard him take the stairs in two bounds and start to wrestle with the gun safe.

"Darling, call the police. Don't go out!" She screamed.

"You call, I'm going to have the bastards. " The front door slammed and she heard him calling wrathfully on the dog to shut its racket and come to him. She picked up the strangely dead receiver and gazed in wonder out of the window as her naked husband ran into view clutching a gun and followed by his dog, before vanishing round the corner of the byre. Suddenly, there were two gunshots and the collie reappeared sprinting madly back towards the house.

"Oh John!" She wailed. Several minutes later, he came marching back, stopping only to shout at the dog.

"Bloody wimp! You were meant to chase them!" He came inside and slammed the door. "They're all gone! Every beast! I never saw a thing. I ran down to the road end but there was no sign of vehicles. All I heard was hoof beats! Christ Almighty! Where are the police?"

"The 'phone's dead" She responded.

"Bloody hell, I hope the insurance covers it. I'll need to speak to the bank in the morning and that useless prick of a bobby!"

Galphay was ecstatic. "There!" He announced looking proudly at the cattle that were starting to settle under the watchful gaze of the entire Coretec contingent. "Now he'll have to feed us. And there are more than we had!" He announced with pride. "Right, that was more in the Coretec spirit. We make our own luck!" He gazed proudly at the stolen herd and whistled a strange little tune. Behind him, his senior managers raised silent eyebrows and pursed lips. Usually, this type of mood led to a major change in policy direction and, while this often led to stunning success it equally often ended in failure and the singling out of some innocent as responsible and therefore to blame. With the benefit of the lessons learned over the long years of survival, they surreptitiously eyed one another for signs of weakness and tried to remember who had attracted Galphay's attention recently. Realising that they had all failed to shine on the course led to further consideration. Finally, they all visibly brightened. Pretending to ignore the whistling presence in front of them, Finance remarked

"Good thinking of Wear's earlier today."

"Absolutely!" A colleague agreed. "Several times we would have been lost without him."

"Guys all know it too, found food, tents, cattle! He's turning out better than I expected." The whistling stopped as Operations called Wear over.

"Here, John, what do you think of the herd?" Unsuspecting, Wear moved to join them and Galphay cocked an ear and whistled gently on.

Chapter 13

Police Constable Findlay had been working for eighteen hours when he finally reached his bed. After a day spent trying to stop tourists totally blocking the villages in his area with badly parked cars, he had followed up a report that a poaching gang would be netting the river. When he finally returned home, he had little doubt that he had been set up so that he would be disinclined to bother going out the following night. As he crawled exhausted under the duvet, he had to accept that the tactic was working. Accordingly, the understandably noisy arrival of Hungry Knowe to report the theft of his cattle was greeted with a certain degree of scepticism by the exhausted constable. "No vehicle? Are you absolutely certain?"

"Of course I'm bloody certain, you moron!"

"Now, now, John, I am only trying to establish the facts." Realising that he sounded like one of the dinosaur country officers he was determined not become, he held up a calming hand. "Come in and have a coffee, I need one and we can get the facts down. I'll put a call out to the traffic boys to keep their eyes open in case there was a cattle float somewhere nearby!" Hungry Knowe was not really in a state where a cup of coffee was going to calm him and let Findlay know.

"For God's sake man, can you not get out looking?" Findlay sighed

"I will be out as soon as I establish all the facts from you and get them out to the rest of the force. Obviously I'll investigate but I need the basic facts."

When Hungry Knowe had left, still cursing over Findlay's admonitions for firing a gun at the intruders, a fact that had emerged during the course of their conversation, the constable had radioed in a report on the theft of ninety pedigree cattle and a request that a watch be kept for unknown lorries in the area. In his opinion, the cattle would be long gone South. He had not

102

mentioned the claims of horses in the dark; well aware that he was already viewed with suspicion by his superiors and that this would merely prove he was unbalanced. He knew that his colleagues failed to appreciate that a First Class degree in law might lead one to wanting to be a policeman rather than a lawyer. It had been rapidly decided that he was too damned clever and he had been quietly shunted off to this backwater in the hope that he would grow bored and resign. After hurriedly consuming a bacon sandwich and a pot of strong coffee, he finished dressing and headed off for Hungry Knowe.

When he arrived, he spoke briefly to the farmer and his wife and walked wearily over to the field where the cattle had been grazing. Hungry Knowe had been carefully dictating the crime number to his insurance company and preparing to contact the authorities to report the unlicensed moving of cattle. Knowing that bureaucracy would keep the unfortunate farmer fully occupied for several hours, he intended to quietly prove that a vehicle had been involved and establish what direction it had taken. He quartered the field like a good hunting spaniel before standing looking at the muddy ground around an open gate. Over the marks of the cattle were overlaid several hoof prints. It seemed Hungry Knowe had been telling the truth. "Bloody marvellous!" Findlay cursed, well aware that his superiors would think his imagination was working overtime. He followed the variety of hoof marks as they crossed the field and through another gate. Finally, the trail arrived where the fence had been broken down and vanished into a wood. Fascinated despite himself, Findlay followed it into the wood. Eventually, the trail ended abruptly on rocky ground and, despite his best efforts, he was unable to pick it up again. Deciding that they must have loaded both cattle and horses onto a float, he headed back to the farmhouse.

Mid morning found Fang carrying out umpiring duties again. On visiting the Fireflow camp, Fang was impressed when they showed him the increased herd and dragged out their prisoners for him to view. "Caught them with their trousers down!" Mickley informed him gleefully.

"So, it went well?" Fang enquired. "Nothing funny happened or anything?" Mickley smiled nastily.

"Only funny thing was that we made a clean sweep including that shower." He nodded in the direction of the prisoners.

"Ah, yes, them. What are you planning on doing with them?" Mickley gazed stonily at the prisoners who tried not to catch his eye.

"Tempting though it is to lose them, I suppose we'll ransom them. Embarrass the blighter." Fang noted the unpleasant tones in which "Lose them" had been uttered and looked closely at Mickley who he had always regarded as the saner of the two Managing Directors.

"I hope that was a joke" He felt compelled to observe. Mickley merely looked at him in response and Fang wondered what had happened to the urbane individual he had first met. "Well, I'll leave you to work out how they can ransom them if you lifted all the cattle." He observed. Mickley grinned again.

"We'll see. Now, I believe we are due extra food?" After explaining that the food would be delivered later, Fang left for Coretec.

On arrival, he was rather disconcerted to find that Coretec were also demanding extra rations as they had doubled the size of their herd. "How the hell can you have done that if Fireflow ran all yours off?" He demanded.

"I don't know about that, but you can see that we've got twice the number of cattle as we did before, so more grub!"

Fang agreed that was fair and promised that it would be delivered shortly. "Saw some of your people over at Fireflow earlier" He remarked, purely to see how Galphay reacted.

"Did you? I sent them to explain to Mickley how to do the bloody job properly. That bugger needs all the help he can get and we want a bit of competition!" Fang sighed. Between them, Mickley and Galphay managed to totally obfuscate the situation and he was none the wiser as to how they both had increased their cattle holdings in a single night.

Returning to Bleakhope, Fang set about sorting the rubbish sacks for hauling down to the gates at the estate entrance to be collected, a weekly chore that he hated, when he heard the hapless local DJ burbling inanely on the radio. Fang was normally irritated by Alice's liking for the local radio station, which he found crass, bland and horribly provincial, but on this occasion the DJ mentioned cattle thefts in the area. Despite himself, Fang paid attention and listened as the minimal facts were produced. For some reason, the report troubled him. Why, he did not know, but intuition told him it involved Bleakhope and the mad bastards he had training. How else could both sides have more cattle than when they had started? Cursing, he walked back to the house to discuss the likelihood of Coretec or Fireflow spreading their wings.

"Don't be silly!" Alice informed him sounding vaguely like a primary school teacher. "Why would they steal cattle? I mean it's..."Her voice trailed off as doubt entered her mind. "Oh, Ian, they wouldn't, surely?"

Fang nodded grimly. "Yes, they're mad enough to do anything!" He was fortunately unaware that his words would prove prophetic. They considered the possibilities for a few minutes before Fang decided that he would warn both companies of the need to remain within the law when he next visited them. Despite himself, he desperately tried to comfort Alice with the view that it was just an unhappy coincidence that cattle had been stolen from a farm bordering the estate. The inconvenient doubling of cattle numbers he tried to ignore despite the sense of growing panic.

That evening, Findlay decided to try and catch the local poachers out by going to the pub where they would expect him to spend the evening as soon as they heard. Instead, he planned to have two pints and then go to patrol the river and look for any sign that the latter day rustlers who seemed to be operating on his patch had returned. One of the local shopkeepers was having a drink with his wife when Findlay entered and he soon joined them at their table. They chatted about inconsequential matters for a few minutes before the subject of the stolen cattle came up. "Well. I can't say much about it as we're still investigating, but it would seem the thieves used horses to move the cattle away and to escape McFadden when he chased them! Quite like old times if you think of it." After a second drink, Findlay left to spend another tiring night hunting poachers and listening for the sound of hoof beats in the night without avail. The poachers were too aware of how the authorities operated traditionally not to watch the pub closely. While he wandered the darkened countryside, he did not know his remark had stirred things up.

A holidaying journalist had been quietly enjoying a bar meal and had overheard the conversation between Findlay and the shopkeeper. Being blessed with a good imagination and always enjoying a story, the journalist rapidly composed a report in his mind and, after finishing his meal, went out to the car park to use his mobile away from potential listeners. His editor was amused at the thought of "The Ghosts of the Reivers Returning" and gave the story prominence on a light news day. Meanwhile, the shopkeeper and his wife who were notorious gossips, wasted no time regaling all who entered the bar with the news that the cattle thieves that had raided Hungry Knowe were on horseback. McFadden and his wife appeared seeking a consoling drink and confirmed that the thieves had indeed ridden off. One of the Divinity students from the scout camp called in to buy a carry out of beer for himself and his friend and, over hearing the discussion, joined in while enjoying a quick pint. Before he left, he mentioned that there were some unpleasant sods riding round the Bleakhope estate although he was careful not to mention the scouts' involvement as he had promised the minister not too in case it raised issues regarding their safe running of the camp.

By the time Fang, Alice and Sonya wandered in for a quiet drink; the locals were in a distinctly unfriendly state. "What the hell are you lot playing at?" Demanded McFadden.

"I beg your pardon, I'm only wanting a drink" Replied a nonplussed Fang.

"No in the bar, on your estate! Bloody people galloping around stealing my cattle!"

"I haven't stolen anyone's cattle!" Fang declared with absolute honesty and total deviousness.

"I didn't mean you had, I meant those effing lunatics you've got staying!"

Fang sighed. "Look, I heard you had had your herd stolen. I'm really sorry but I don't see what it's got to do with a Management Training course we are running on the estate. Yes, they're riding, carrying out exercises like night navigation, but they're not cattle rustlers and they stay on our ground!" This robust defence quietened the situation but the trio soon drank up and left as the atmosphere remained distinctly hostile and the arrival of more farmers served to inflame McFadden again. As the door shut behind them, they heard the shopkeeper's wife announce loudly "They're involved somehow! Toffs are all the same, so long as they're alright the rest of us can go to hell!"

Fang looked at the girls. "Looks like we'll be drinking at home in the future and shopping elsewhere!"

As Fang and the girls wandered worriedly back up the long drive in the dark, they heard a faint drumming of hooves and stopped to listen. The sound faded away as they stood, and soon the only noise was the gentle night breeze stirring the vegetation. Fang cursed, it would seem both Coretec and Fireflow were trying to gain the upper hand and had riders out in force. He only hoped they would concentrate on each other, rather than trying to involve the local population, but he held out little hope that this would be the case. "Bugger it!" Fang announced. "Either they start being sensible or we'll have to close the training down." He sighed loudly. "Just think of all the money we'll lose though!"

Alice pointed out the flaw in his reasoning. "If we close the course down, the locals will see that as an admission of guilt! We've got to calm Coretec and Fireflow and run it to its end. Otherwise, nasty rumours will be seen as fact!"

"Well, they are. Fact I mean!" Fang pointed out. "We can't deny we've tried to re enact the reivers or that we've brought two bands of lunatics together. Christ, I hope McFadden believed me!" Sonya remained silent.

"What do you think Sonya?" Alice asked, vaguely hoping for comfort.

"Well, from what I know, both companies are intensely driven, goal orientated and, from the signs, just getting into the whole training thing." This statement did not add to the others peace of mind.

"Just getting into? Just getting into? How far do you want them to go?" Fang yelled. Alice just gazed horror struck at her friend.

"I think that we need to quieten them down" Sonya stated.

"I agree, if we close things down as soon as the locals point a finger, it will be seen as proof that the rustlers came from our course. Equally, I think both Coretec and Fireflow have got too into the whole role-play. They need reminding it isn't real and that they are hear to learn."

"Oh bugger!" Fang announced and they started walking once more.

The next morning saw the publication of the "The Return of the Ghost Reivers." It was read with interest by many and its effect was almost instant with regard to several of those wittingly or unwittingly involved in the drama. The first that Constable Findlay knew was when he received a furious telephone call from Head Quarters demanding to know the meaning of the story. On his replying that he did not know what they were talking about, the voice of higher command censured him for not being aware of the crime being committed in his area. Once he established that the voice was referring to the recent incident of cattle rustling, he pointed out that he had indeed been endeavouring to solve the matter and had reported the need to watch for unknown cattle floats and the like the previous morning. "And when did you report the Ghost Reivers?" stopped him in his tracks.

"Ghost reivers?" He queried desperately.

"This rag quotes police sources in the area saying that the cattle thieves used horses just like their ancestors the reivers. You're the closest thing to a policeman that we have in the area, so what did you tell the press, Constable?" Findlay felt that his claims never to have spoken to the press were not believed. He had just put down the receiver when a thunderous knocking on the door heralded the arrival of McFadden.

While Findlay desperately tried to point out to McFadden that the fact that there were trainees riding around the Bleakhope Estate did not mean that they were necessarily cattle rustlers or that Fang was organising games for his rich friends at the expense of poor farmers, he realised to his horror that several cars had turned up and were disgorging various people who could only be journalists in view of the Dictaphones and notebooks that they bore. He retreated inside as the first camera flashed, capturing him dragging a protesting McFadden with him. The journalists were unhappy having been beaten to the story by a little respected Scottish paper and were seeking any angle they could find. At that moment they could see "Wrongful arrest" and "Police arrest complainant" as easy options. The reappearance of McFadden rather spoiled those ideas but they chased him down the road back to his farm where the dog at least restored its position by fending them off so that he could escape inside his home.

Fang had woken early worrying about how best to rein in the wilder excesses of Fireflow and Coretec. He had rapidly decided that the girls were correct in their view that to cut the course short would be to admit guilt, but how to regain control eluded him. The arrival of the first journalist who had picked up on the story that a local landlord was organising games for his rich friends that were bankrupting hard working locals, did not improve his outlook. Having vehemently denied any wrong doing, unless the journalist felt that running a training course was an illegal act, he had stonewalled all further questions until the journalist, deciding that he would gain no more information, left. Before setting off to try and sort out the trainees, Fang had shut and bolted the main gates in the hope of deterring further visits from the press. He then pondered over the journalist's mention of the published story not bearing out the facts and had visited the village to check the papers for any mention of either the estate or cattle rustling. The shopkeeper's attitude was such that he found himself unable to search each paper but landed up purchasing one of each to check back at the house. Leaving to disapproving looks, he was accosted by another journalist who informed him it was interesting how often the guilty liked to read about them selves. He did not help his cause by losing his temper, but neither did the journalist gain a further insight into events other than the fact that Fang was not a good man to cross.

The previous night had seen Coretec out hoping to ambush further raids by Fireflow and gain hostages of their own but to no avail. As a result, they were tired and irritable. Fireflow, in turn, despite the best efforts of Sales to scout a way past Coretec's defences, had failed to reach their objective and were equally tired and felt that they had missed an opportunity to gain further points, although they were pleased that they had been undetected. The Forty Third Glasgow Scouts were still smarting from the loss of their food and tents despite the Reverend McLeod having replaced their stores and obtained new tents. Generally, they felt that they had not yet extracted proper revenge for their troubles. The early morning sun emphasised the dark forbidding stone of Bleakhope tower.

Chapter 14

It took Fang a considerable time to persuade Alice and Sonya to agree to visit both Coretec and Fireflow to inform them that a Warden's day was to take place. "Look, I appreciate that they make you uneasy but nobody has tried to pinch or grope you since the first day." He waited for Alice's diatribe against the swine they were training to ramble to a stop. "If I go, it rather weakens my claim to control them doesn't?" Despite herself Alice agreed. "You alright with that Sonya?" He enquired.

"Oh yes, give me a chance to gauge their mood and so on. Might get a useful insight. Also, if we visit together it should reduce the risk of any incidents. Anyway, they'll probably be too tired to get frisky." Fang refrained from enquiring if Sonya had found trainees getting randy on previous courses she had run. Alice merely asked her when they were alone and was unsurprised by the answer.

Both Fireflow and Coretec reacted badly to being informed that they had to attend another Warden's day. "Hardly got going!" Mickley grumbled. "I mean, chaps are getting into the swing of it and we keep stopping to chat. Can't you just speak to the oiks?" Galphay was at his most charming by way of contrast, spitting eloquently at their feet. "I'll take that as agreement then." Alice informed him icily. As they walked back to their ponies, Sonya observed loudly to Alice

"Fake aggression is often a sign of impotence you know."

"Really?"

"Oh yes. I've been disappointed too often not to recognise the signs." Leaving Galphay swearing nastily to himself, they rode away.

Over coffee, Fang asked Sonya if she felt she had learned anything during their visits. "Not sure, really. Both Mickley and Coretec are control freaks, won't let anyone else speak on their behalf, but I'd expect that anyway. Both are still holding to their original way of working, Fireflow are all organisation, planning and do it this way, meaning Mickley's or get out. Coretec just work on aggression and the pack principle. I'd say they would take any losses if it meant they would ultimately win."

"I hope you mean financial!" Fang remarked.

"Oh, if it came down to it, losses of any sort wouldn't really bother Galphay. I'd say they are both quite formidable in their way. And determined."

"Bloody marvellous! So they're barking, determined to succeed and see obstacles as something to be removed?" Sonya considered briefly.

"Yes, that sums them up rather well." Fang put his face in his hands and started to rock gently in his chair. The girls hoped he was joking.

Before setting off to meet the two factions, Fang was struggling to think of them as trainees anymore, the trio discussed the best approach and what Fang needed to ensure with regard to the future conduct of both parties. "They've got to understand that they can only operate within the estate and lift each others cattle. I'll point out that the press and the police, not to mention the locals are all sniffing around!" Fang announced.

"Yes, and don't forget to point out that assaulting children and stealing their food and shelter is not part of the course!" Alice stated. Sonya listened and said nothing until Fang and Alice looked at her.

"Well?" Fang demanded.

"Well," Sonya replied, "I'm not sure what your best approach would be. If you are too dictatorial, they may decide to ignore you, to conciliatory and they'll decide you're not worth listening to. Bit of a problem really." Fang erupted.

"For God's sake, you make them sound like a pair of criminal gangs not companies on a training course!"

"Absolutely." Sonya replied, then laughed at the look of horror on Fang and Alice's faces. "Look, I'm only joking. They, that is Galphay and Mickley, are not used to being told what to do so they'll be as awkward as possible. You need to be firm but not over the top. Point out that they are making themselves look stupid and they'll soon stop!" Fang felt reassured by this authoritative statement, not knowing how wrong Sonya was.

As they approached the meeting place, Fang felt strangely restless, and kept turning in his saddle, as if looking for something. Former inhabitants of Bleakhope would have recognised the behaviour for what it was, the basic survival instinct sensing the possibility of violence from an unknown source. Fang did not, so he rode on but with an increasing sense of being watched. Finally, he reined his pony in. "Sorry" He informed Alice and Sonya. "I've decided to meet them on my own. You should go back to the house and wait for me there." They looked at him in astonishment.

"But I like seeing you sort them out!" Alice announced.

"Not today, " Fang informed her. "I'd just be happier if the two of you were away from here." Despite their protests he remained adamant. Finally, he lost his temper. "Just do what your asked for God's sake! I don't need to be watched all the time in case I go wrong. I'm just going to be telling these idiots that they need to behave." The girls departed in a marked fashion and failed to notice the Coretec riders who watched them silently from the trees.

Now admitting to himself he felt nervous, Fang rode on. As he proceeded, he felt as if he was being watched by unseen eyes and, despite reminding himself that it was the twenty first century, felt sweat trickling between his shoulder blades. In a way, it was a strange relief to reach the meeting place and he sat his pony looking around the silent field. Surely to God they'll turn up, he wondered, but there was no sign of either party. He lent forward and slapped a horsefly that had settled on his pony's neck and it was as if the noise had summoned Coretec and Fireflow. Both suddenly swept over the low ridge to either side of Fang, and cantered down to rein in on either side of him. He noted that both had come from the opposite direction to that which he had anticipated and that they were all much better at riding even after such a short time. As he waited for both sides to settle, Fang could not help noticing that they had changed dramatically from the start of the course the previous Sunday. Obviously, a lot of the men were showing considerable stubble and one or two were developing beards, but it was more the easy way they all sat at ease on their ponies, had altered their clothing to make riding easier, and were developing unpleasantly steady stares that he found disconcerting. He definitely preferred the confused, nervous and disorientated trainees of Sunday rather than hard bitten looking ruffians that now surrounded him. Taking a deep breath, Fang got proceedings underway.

"Right!" He announced. "As I've said before, some of you are fast forgetting that this is training! I need to remind you that attacking and stealing from children is not acceptable or part of the course!" He took a deep breath to shout over the rising chorus of disagreement from Coretec. "Further, the lifting of pedigree cattle from neighbouring farms who have nothing to do with us is just not on!" He was conscious that his words lacked the necessary gravitas, but pressed on. "You need to take the cattle back!" Coretec's reaction was much as he had anticipated. To a man and woman, they roared and screamed defiance at him while edging their ponies closer. Fang glared furiously back at their contorted faces. "Just for your information, you stupid bastards, the police and the press are all over the place trying to work out who's guilty. Right now, they've even been on the estate asking questions!" Instead of quietening them, this statement seemed to enrage them further and for a moment, Fang thought that they were going to attack him as a mob and lynch him. As he prepared to go down fighting, Galphay reined his supporters back with a bellowed

"Shut it you bastards!" He then looked closely at Fang. "The press and the police are sniffing around?" Thank God, Fang thought for a moment, he sees the problem. His hopes were immediately dashed.

"Yes, they bloody are!" Fang snapped.

"Well, you'd better keep them away, or I'll string you up by your bollocks!" Despite himself, Fang gulped. There was a terrible sincerity to Galphay's words that were distinctly chilling. His feelings were not helped when he heard Mickley.

"If this is true, I will make sure he cannot carry out his threat. I shall have gelded you!" Fang would have crossed his legs tightly if he had not been on horseback.

"Of course it's fucking true!" He yelled at Mickley, "The problem is stopping them looking any deeper and finding you and your fellow lunatics are actually behind what has been going on! Don't blame me if you are demented lunatics with the morals of a snake!" Mickley had calmed again.

"How eloquent. In any event, we at Fireflow have nothing to fear from the law or the press, unlike those, ah, people" He waved a languid hand in the vague direction of Coretec. This had the effect of diverting attention from Fang, for which he was truly grateful.

Watching the two sides bellow at one another, Fang's temper, despite the cold sweat of fear that stood on his brow, reasserted itself. While a small inner voice whimpered, he kicked his pony into a trot between the two sides, turned and trotted back, forcing them marginally further apart. "Enough of this crap!" He yelled. "I shall not be threatened on my own land! Now listen!" To their mutual astonishment, Coretec and Fireflow did as they were told. Far in the distance, a bunch of hoodie crows rose above Bleakhope tower as if suddenly startled.

While Fang was explaining the nuances of what was and was not acceptable within the parameters of the Training, Sonya and Alice were startled when the crows rose loudly into the air. "What are they bothered about?" Sonya wondered.

"I don't know. I wish Ian had let us stay." Alice informed her.

"Well, he's probably right about getting on better if we're not there." Alice sighed; she did not want to admit that watching Fang dominating Fireflow and Coretec exciting or watching him beat up Galphay a positive turn on. Instead, she pointed up at the tower.

"We might see what's happening from up there." She remarked hopefully.

"Worth a try." Sonya agreed and they made their way over to the tower. Unseen the spaniel moved toward the gate and looked South in the direction Fang had taken. High above, the girls could see little other than a vague blob that was probably the Warden meeting. "I wonder what's happening." Sonya queried.

What was happening, was that Coretec had demanded the return of their colleagues who had been lifted together with their cattle by Fireflow. Fireflow unsurprisingly refused to accede to this demand. Further, they refocused attention on Fang by appealing for him to rule in their favour. Fang had just realised that his diatribe had calmed both sides and had been preparing to quietly remove himself from the vicinity when they started arguing amongst themselves. Now, he was the centre of attention again as they all stared at him awaiting his judgement. He sighed knowing that he was going to set things off once more. "Right, I did say that you could make full use of your ingenuity to do better than the other side. Bearing in mind that hostage taking was a regular tactic of the Reivers that seems a fair solution. How your going to pay for them is up to you!" It was the female members of Coretec who reacted first, for some reason immediately assuming that the hostages be returned based on what they might offer. While Fang gazed on them in stunned disbelief, their colleagues also shouted their disagreement with this attempt at judgement. Fang raised himself in his stirrups to shout louder, but the mob as he now thought of them, continued to bay their disapproval. Try as he might, Fang was unable to make himself heard over the cacophony. The situation grew even worse when Fireflow started chanting,

"Pay! Pay!" With admirable determination and not a little of the stubbornness for which his ancestors had been famed, Fang continued to try and make himself heard, but to no avail. Finally, he realised that he had lost control and, indeed any authority that he might have had. He decided that he might as well leave them to it and catch Galphay on his own later and turned his mount away from the crowd. He had only moved away about twenty metres, when he heard the first shouts.

"Get the cheating bastard!" He glanced over his shoulder and saw Coretec kicking their ponies out of the throng in his direction.

"Bloody hell" He announced and lashed his pony with the reins, startling it into a gallop.

Soon, Fang was desperately trying to keep ahead of a pack of Coretec riders who were riding furiously in his wake. They pounded across two fields with no sign of the pursuers keenness abating and Fang realised that there was every chance that they would catch him if he did not try to slow the pursuit somehow and win some distance. Yelling encouragement at his pony, he swerved towards a dry stone wall and kicked on. As soon as his beast landed, he kicked it on again and glanced over his shoulder. Unfortunately, with only two exceptions, Coretec took the wall in fine style still in hot pursuit. Next, Fang rode for the protection of a small wood and ducked low as his mount galloped into the trees. Curses and at least one yell of dismay gave him hope and he came out the far side only to rein savagely round and dive back into the trees once more. This tactic slowed Coretec, the faster riders turning into the face of the slower so that they were brought to a standstill as they tried to avoid colliding with each other and the trees. Fang meantime, had swung once more for home and what he hoped was safety.

Up on the roof of the tower, Alice and Sonya had grasped that Fang was being chased by the hard riding Coretec contingent. "Oh God!" Alice wailed. "They've gone mad!" Sonya stared in horror at the unfolding tragedy. The fastest of the pursuers were trying to cut Fang off from the sanctuary of Bleakhope, while he was desperately encouraging his tiring pony to try and outpace them. Falling back slightly, but still following, the slower were still chasing their prey hard. Suddenly, uttering a yell of defiance, Fang reined round hard and rode furiously back at the main body of Coretec, momentarily removing the fastest riders from the equation. Fang was gambolling that the more faint hearted or less committed of Coretec made up the following pack and he was proved correct as they desperately avoided colliding with him as he rode full tilt at them. Not unnaturally, they spilt in two and within seconds, ponies and riders were swerving in all directions as they tried to avoid Fang and then their more committed colleagues who had doubled back in hot pursuit. Once more Fang turned his now exhausted pony for home, knowing he could only hope it could keep going long enough. The gunshots startled them all into a faltering stop.

Alice had overcome her hysterics to run down the stairs, across the yard and into the house where she had unlocked the gun cabinet and run back outside clutching two shotguns and a half empty box of cartridges. Handing one weapon to Sonya she had sprinted out into the field towards Fang as his pony laboured towards her. She stopped, flanked by Sonya, and loaded her gun. Sonya had followed suit and then Alice had fired twice into the air as the pursuit galloped towards her. The sheer noise recalled Coretec to the modern day and they looked almost shamefaced as they gazed at the wild eyed Alice and then at Sonya before considering a white faced Fang who had slid off his exhausted pony. The Coretec riders looked at each other then back at Fang and his supporters. Several shook their heads and, acting as one, they reined round and started back the way they had come. The spaniel, evilly loyal, scurried forward, it was later thought that it had probably been looking for shot game, and nipped at Galphay's pony's heels so that it suddenly broke into a gallop nearly unseating him with several fly kicks as it went. The rest of Coretec followed their leader as fast as they could. The spaniel sat down and scratched itself vigorously.

When Coretec returned to the meeting place, they found Fireflow were still waiting to discuss the hostages. Neither side saw any need to mention Fang, although several of Fireflow carefully studied the opposition for bloodstains on their hands or clothing. "Right," Mickley announced "You can buy them back at four head of cattle each!" This immediately led to a volley of oaths from Galphay before the two settled down to some hard bargaining. Their supporters sat their ponies in silence watching and listening. Gradually, through a chorus of "Look Old Boy" and "Listen you soft bugger" it became apparent that they were edging towards agreement. Finally, it was agreed that the hostages would be exchanged for two head of cattle each and it was agreed that they exchange would take place at the river. Considerable haggling then took place as to how the exchange was to take place without either side being cheated. Finally it was thrashed out that six Fireflow riders would escort the hostages who would be tied to their saddles and an equal number from Coretec would herd the cattle. The exchange would take place when they met in the middle of the river at sundown.

In the event, the seeming agreement came to nothing. Coretec duly turned up at the appointed place and time with eight cattle to retrieve their colleagues. They were met by only one Fireflow rider, who bluntly told them the hostages refused to be ransomed. "We've tried everything" He assured the furious Galphay "But they say they got properly fed and it's more comfortable! Nothing more we can do. Keep the cattle, we'll collect them another time!" Leaving a raging Galphay vociferously supported by his followers in his bellows of "Cheating bastards!" The Fireflow messenger rode off. He reported that Coretec had taken the news badly, indeed the last thing he had heard was Galphay swearing he would have revenge. Mickley laughed.

"Let him try." He announced baldly.

Chapter 15

Wear had not been enjoying life following being set up by the senior management team. Galphay never missed an opportunity to belittle him and his position as the butt of their leader's unpleasant humour had rapidly led the rest to award him white crow status. As a result he found that any unpleasant jobs were allocated to him without compunction. He was well aware that this was unlikely to change in the future and that any hopes he had previously held of having a career with Coretec were over before they had really begun. It was, he supposed, typical of Galphay that he would assume that anyone treated as Wear had been would remain loyal to the company until he was fired. It was not as if he would be unable to find another job he reassured himself. With a sigh, he headed over to where the ponies were corralled and collected his mount and saddled up. It was tempting to just keep going, vanish without trace by riding away or cross to Fireflow and betray what Coretec was planning but he knew he wouldn't do it. Firstly. He needed to get his car, collect his bag of modern necessities such as wallet, mobile phone and house keys from Fang and secondly, what information could he offer Fireflow? No one would ever find it difficult to work out what Galphay was planning, his attempts at deviousness made a six year old seem sly and cunning. The one thing about Galphay was his willingness to bull doze whatever opposition stood in his path. With a heartfelt sigh, Wear swung into the saddle and went to scout for signs of Fireflow in the area.

Alison Sweetness was as equally disillusioned with life in the Fireflow camp as Wear was with his lot. Ever since she had subdued the ponies, her colleagues had let their dislike for her show. It stemmed, she reckoned, from Mickley's dislike of being proved wrong. He had obviously expected her to be humiliated when trying to ride the pony and she had succeeded. The work force was finely tuned to Mickley's moods and had lost no time in spotting that he no longer regarded her with favour. Accordingly, they never let an opportunity pass to annoy or snub her. She had started to ride out alone, essentially rambling around the Bleakhope estate where the fancy took her. She also spent the time spotting various players as they went about their business. For instance, she knew that Wear was the most frequent spy sent out by Coretec, that the Forty Third Glasgow scouts saw nearly everything that happened from hidden places and that Alice and Fang had a very active sex life. Seemingly inattentive, she drifted across the estate, seldom moving out of dead ground or out of the shadows. She spotted Wear after about an hour and quietly stood her pony in the shadow of a patch of hawthorns waiting.

Wear was doing his best to be both inconspicuous and watchful. Secretly, he rather enjoyed the role of lone scout seeking signs of the enemy and was proud of what he thought of as his skills in the role. He nearly screamed embarrassingly when Alison Sweetness spoke from just behind him. "Seen anything?" She enquired. Wear twisted round to look at her.

"Christ, Alison, you nearly gave me a heart attack!"

"You should pay more attention then. Anyway, why are you pottering about?"

"I'm supposed to be looking for you lot about to mount a raid on the cattle. At least it gives me a chance to be on my own" He knew he sounded bitter and waited for Sweetness to pounce on the sign of weakness. Instead she surprised him.

"You too? Bunch of pricks aren't they?" They sighed in unison.

"I take it things are slightly different than what you had hoped?" Wear enquired.

"Just a bloody bit!" She responded. "You?" Wear gazed up at the sky

"I was thinking of jacking." He informed her.

"That good? Fancy a drink?"

"What? Here?" She laughed.

"Nah, at the pub in the village. Come on, be a change from sodding around on your own." Wear laughed at the thought.

"True, but I've no money, it's all back at that castle." Sweetness smiled almost beguilingly.

"Well, I hid some cash before II turned up. You must have read the details as much as me and spotted that we were meant to rough it probably meant no money?" Wear did not want to admit that he had not interpreted the brochure as meaning no money but did not want to admit it. Instead, her smiled.

"Lead on!"

The Fireflow picket spotted the two figures running towards them while they were still far out and, as one circled to signal someone unknown was approaching the camp, the rest rode out to intercept them Once they realised that it was two scouts, they let them follow them back to the camp. They refused to say what they wanted unless they were allowed to see the boss. At first, the programmers who were on picket duty, struggled to understand what the boys were saying, but after Jamesie shouted a bit they grasped that they had news for the 'heid bummer'. Once Mickley was fetched, he seemed to have no problem understanding or being understood by, Jamesie and his colleague. "Well, you chaps got news?"

"Aye, yon wee lass is aff tae rah boozer wi' wan o' yon scum!"

"Intriguing! Well done chaps. Anything else? No? Well, we'll get you some steaks to take back to your camp and toddle down to the village to see what's up." Once the scouts had left clutching a bloody parcel, Mickley shed his bonhomie. "Right! Saddle up. We can teach that little madam a lesson and take her boyfriend hostage. Come along!"

Coretec was an unhappy organisation, riven with unhappiness, distrust and opportunism regarding gaining notice by senior management and, more importantly, Galphay. Unsurprisingly, Wear's willingness to carry out lone patrols had raised suspicion amongst some of the staff. Only Galphay's P.A. bothered to do anything about it, and followed Wear at a discrete distance. She was pleasantly surprised to actually spot something happening that she could report back, missing her normal power as gatekeeper to the Managing Director, and she relished the opportunity to remind Galphay of her worth. She watched and trailed the pair as they rode talking animatedly together and, in Sweetness' case showing an unusual lack of caution. Once she observed them tether their ponies, grub around the base of a tree then climb a fence and walk towards the village pub, she headed back to base as fast as she could make her pony gallop. She wasn't disappointed by

Galphay's reaction or the praise he heaped on her. Within minutes, Coretec were in the saddle and thundering towards the village.

The Sluggish Trout was busy that night. Apart form the regulars in the pub the local National Farmers Union were holding their monthly meeting. The main topic, despite the combined efforts of the chairman and the guest speaker, a garrulous Northumbrian from an animal feeds firm, was the theft of the cattle from Hungry Knowe and the possible identity of the criminals. As the evening passed and drinks were consumed, the mood of the farmers gradually hardened from defeated to bloody minded. "We should set up patrols and just sort the buggers when we catch them Leave the polis out of it!" A chorus of ayes rumbled around the bar. The guest speaker held forth on how his ancestors had administered swift justice on cattle thieves in the past and only slowly realised he was probably talking about the gathering's ancestors. Several eyed him speculatively and he suddenly found his pint interesting. "Well." The chairman tried to resurrect the planned discussion on additives that might aid cattle growth, "What d'you think Archie?" Archie stared glassily into the fire and finished his whisky.

"I think I'll have another, thank you chairman." The chairman sighed and took the proffered glass. He had not realised the expense involved in his role before taking up post.

Wear and Alison Sweetness were ensconced in a corner, happily absorbed in each other's company. Unsurprisingly, their unhappy state, combined with their previous alliance, made them relax. In a surprising change from her former ruthless exploitation of his physical interest, now she snuggled up against him and encouraged him to tell her of his problems. Wear, despite previous experience and the likelihood of being both disillusioned and frustrated in equal measure in the near future, decided to enjoy the moment. Accordingly, the time passed quickly and they grew ever more absorbed in one another. Wear finally decided to push his luck and kissed her and she was responding enthusiastically when Fireflow pushed into the bar. The sudden silence finally gained the couple's attention and they disengaged to see what was happening. They both gazed in horror at the glowering faces that surrounded them. Sweetness gave a small squeak and tried to hide behind Wear who, deciding he was going to be thumped and might as well get a punch or two in first, stood up and prepared to take a swing at Mickley. Just then, the door crashed open and Galphay marched in while the rest of Coretec pressed in behind. Both sides turned to glare at one another and the NFU members sat back to enjoy the show. "Get us another, lad," commanded Archie. "But be quick before they shut the bar!" The chairman set off to comply.

"What the bloody hell are you doing with that nasty little bint?" Galphay enquired. Wear had moved to a state of recklessness and also felt that Alison Sweetness was as close to a girlfriend as he had had since leaving university.

"Bugger off!" he responded with feeling.

"Just wait your turn you oaf!" Mickley told Galphay as he started to turn red. "You really should learn manners! Now, you!" he pointed at Sweetness. "Explain yourself!" One of the farmers burst into fits of laughter.

"Better than a soap!" he announced happily.

"You can bugger off as well!" A now furious Wear informed Mickley. This had the effect of causing the farmers to cheer, enraging Mickley, cemented Alison Sweetness' feelings for him and was the spark that turned a training course into an outbreak of lawlessness on a scale unseen for four hundred years.

Mickley turned crimson with rage and mouthed incoherently before yelling at Wear.

"You little shit! You can't just steal my staff like you do cattle!"

"Just a minute!" Galphay grabbed him by the arm. "Who are you calling a cattle thief?" Before Mickley could do more than snarl,

"You and all your unutterable crew!" the farmers reacted. Archie led the way, snatching his refilled glass from the chairman; he drained it before throwing it at Mickley. Mickley ducked, inadvertently avoiding the punch Galphay had thrown who accidentally hit a fast approaching Hungry Knowe. Uttering an incoherent roar, Hungry Knowe waded into Galphay and Mickley in a flurry of punches. His colleagues were not slow in backing him up and the Guest Speaker quickly set about showing why he had played prop for his county. Fireflow and Coretec were momentarily confused by this attack from an unexpected quarter, but soon decided their mutual hatred could wait in the face of a common foe and threw themselves at the farmers. The remaining drinkers not unnaturally, decided to support their fellow locals against the outsiders. As the first chair and body went through the window as the Guest Speaker built up a head of steam, the landlord, in between flourishing a cricket bat ineffectually from behind the safety of the bar, rang the police. The furious melee surged up and down the room, trampling furniture and the fallen with equal abandon. Hungry Knowe went down under the joint assault of Mickley and Galphay but was saved from further punishment by Archie who appeared swinging the leg of a coffee table broken under the impact of two wrestling bodies. The shopkeeper's wife was having her head pounded on the floor by an infuriated Fireflow Head of Marketing who had suffered a drink being poured over her head. "Peasant!" she screamed in time to the thump of her victim's cranium until a passing farmer cuffed her off. She then joined battle with Mickley's PA. Over the yells, screams and curses, the dull thud of punches landing, groans as boots thudded home and happy yells from the battling guest speaker, the landlord was trying to summon constable Findlay to restore order and save what remained of his house.

"They're destroying the place! Not the antique table, man! What? Who is it? The Sluggish Trout, that's who! Aye, the pub! Bloody great crowd murdering one another and destroying my premises! Get yourself dow..." He slid to the floor clutching his head as Archie, dragging the groaning Hungry Knowe towards the door accidentally caught him one with the table leg he was still swinging wildly to clear his way.

The NFU chairman viewed the scene with distaste, he liked to think that the size of his farm meant he was a gentleman farmer and this was far from gentlemanly. He watched closely as a hard pressed colleague reeled back against the bar under a hail of punches, sighed, placed his pint on the bar and tapped the nearest incomer on the shoulder. Mickley turned to stare at him. "Excuse me," the chairman announced, glancing upwards. Mickley unwisely followed suit and received a butt between the eyes to stagger away clutching his face. The chairman sighed and picked up his glass again.

The fight was surprisingly equal despite the disparity in numbers. The farmers tended to be fitter and certainly stronger which reduced the effect of their lack of numbers. They also felt that they had right on their side and were happy to prove it. The trainees had numbers but somehow lacked the sheer viciousness and durability of their opponents, many of whom had played rugby in their youth. The farmers' ability to absorb punishment and keep on fighting slightly awed some of their opponents so the overall effect was equality.

As the numbers of wounded reduced to lying prostrate, crawling amongst the wreckage or just leaning retching against walls grew, the fight grew more vicious in its intensity as natural selection left the best on each side still standing. Mickley's PA and Coretec's Head of Marketing were almost unrecognizable as one's childhood spent in a family of boys was cancelled out by the others addiction to Boxercise. The Guest Speaker was now to short of breath to utter any more odd Northumbrian yells, but was still swinging punches like a squat machine at Galphay who was returning them with gusto. The chairman, in a strangely feline fashion, sauntered amongst the battling croups, occasionally singling out a victim when he felt the farmer involved was losing. Archie had re-entered the fray having placed Hungry Knowe in the lobby to recover and was fencing furiously with Coretec's Head of Operations as they both wielded table legs. The Sales team from Fireflow were living up to their reputation as hard drinking, hard fighting types against the Young Farmers who had just arrived from a lecture for a quiet pint. It was into this sudden resurgence of fighting, that PC Findlay unwisely stepped.

The first that the combatants knew of the arrival of the police, was a stentorian bellow of "Stop, in the name of the law"! Pausing only to curse himself for yet again sounding old-fashioned, Findlay drew his truncheon and waded into the melee. His first two swings promptly disabled a Coretec and a Fireflow fighter as they flailed at one another, both collapsed clutching the respective shoulder Findlay had targeted proving the efficacy of the tactic. Archie, in the heat of his duel with Coretec's Head of Operations, had failed to notice Findlay's arrival. Seeing only another stick wielding assailant coming at him, he turned and smartly belted Findlay over the head with his table leg. Findlay staggered in a half circle and dropped. The room froze momentarily as they all recognised the fallen figure as wearing police uniform, then erupted into violent movement. Dropping opponents, grabbing fallen colleagues, they jammed struggling in the doors, scrabbled out the windows and vanished into the dark dragging or carrying their wounded with them.

Within thirty seconds, the landlord found himself gazing at the wreckage of a formerly successful business with the nearest thing to a patron, an unconscious policeman lying amongst the debris on the floor. He was still gaping at the scene, when the remains of the front door opened and the chairman of the NFU sauntered in. "Evening," he announced and crossed to the fallen Findlay and carefully moved him into the recovery position. "Been busy?" the chairman enquired looking around the room. The landlord made a strangled noise that could have meant anything. "Quite." The chairman chose to assume this was agreement. He carefully leant against the bar and looked at the landlord.

The landlord became conscious that he was still clutching his cricket bat and placed it under the bar as the chairman viewed him quizzically. "Licence renewal due soon?" The chairman observed. "Awful   bore   reviewing   applications."   he   observed inconsequentially, then looked around the remains of the bar. "Football supporters I suppose?" he wondered. The landlord gazed back. "Take at least two busloads to cause this much damage I'd imagine. Must have been damned unlucky, two team's fans turning up at the same time. Hmm?" The landlord nodded mutely. "Don't suppose you've seen any of the boys tonight have you? No?" The landlord sighed and agreed with the local magistrate that he had not seen any farmers that evening. "Any glasses left for a drink?" the chairman enquired. "No? Oh well, you'd better call for an ambulance and let the Police Headquarters know about that." The landlord gazed after the chairman as he sauntered out the door and sighed.

Fireflow had returned to their tethered ponies and, ignoring those of his employees who lay or crouched groaning and whimpering, Mickley advanced on an unrepentant Sweetness. "Consorting with the enemy! Trusted you! Cherished hopes! You are surplus to requirements! Leave the, ah, animal and go!" He turned his back as Sweetness walked through the glowering throng. They all remembered the unfortunate pony and, despite the opportunity to gain revenge for previous humiliations, chose not to impede her progress. Sweetness glared at them as she left but, other than curling her lip nastily, did not deign to speak. She vanished into the night. "Ungrateful hussy. Now, where are Sales, hmm?" The Head of Sales materialised at his side. "Few loose ends, I think. I will take this, ah, crew, back to base. You had better ensure that the landlord fails to remember anything due to the shock he has suffered." The Head of Sales nodded assent. "You do still have sufficient numbers for the task in hand?" Mickley enquired and received assurance that this was the case.

Coretec gazed at the departing figure of Wear dumfounded. Instead of waiting for Galphay to declare him persona nom grata, he had assisted a tottering Head of Marketing back to the ponies before informing Galphay he could stick his job and walking off. Operations appeared at Galphay's elbow. "D'you want me and the boys to..." Galphay had snorted through his swelling nose courtesy of the guest Speaker.

"No, let the bugger be, we're better without him. I do need you to point out to that landlord we were nowhere near his bloody pub though."

"Right!" Operations called up his men and vanished into the gloom.

The landlord heard the broken door grate open and called, "We're closed!" without looking up.

"Good, then no one will hear our conversation." He swung round to look at Coretec's Head of Operations.

"You! You're barred and just wait 'til the Police get here!" Operations nodded in seeming agreement before responding.

"That's why I wanted a word. Gentlemen?" A painful minute later, the landlord agreed he had never seen the Head of Operations or, indeed, any one other than the football supporters mentioned by the NFU chairman that evening. "I'm so glad we agree," Operations informed him, and they vanished into the night. The landlord looked for an unbroken glass without success and had just taken a mouthful of whisky from a bottle he had found behind the bar, when the door opened once more.

"You took your bloody time, I, oh, you're not the police!" Fireflow's Head of Sales agreed that he and his men were not. "What the bloody hell are they doing?" the landlord enquired desperately as the Sales team flicked lighters on and off.

"I think they are cold and looking to get warm."

"Christ Almighty. You can't!" The Head of Sales smiled warmly.

"We can, but it would be a shame to see such a nice building burn down by accident. However, provided you remember that we have not been on your premises tonight…" He let his words hang. The landlord nodded resentful agreement. "I'm sure you can come up with a convincing explanation. Line dancing or something?" The landlord nodded again, temporarily speechless. "Well, we'll be off then. Pleasure meeting you."

When the Police finally arrived they found the landlord seemingly callously sweeping around the prostrate figure of Constable Findlay, humming too himself in a strange fashion. This did not endear him to the Inspector or his sergeant. Nor did his tale of rival football fans turning up unexpectedly and having a heated discussion in his pub. "Doesn't ring true, does it?" the Inspector remarked. His deputy agreed.

"If this was the city, I'd be thinking protection and gangs, but here in the sticks? No way, sir!" The Inspector nodded.

"Aye, my views exactly. Take him back and sweat him for a while, see if we can get anything useful out of him." They watched Findlay being carried out the door. "And I don't like seeing policemen, even that thing, being beaten to a pulp. Pressure him sergeant!"

"Sir." The unfortunate landlord was dragged protesting and struggling to a waiting vehicle.

"For God's sake, I'm the bloody victim! Why can't you lot ever…" his voice was cut off sharply and then a door slammed. The Inspector sighed and turned to look at the room although he knew that there would be little he could do without a worthwhile witness and something told him the landlord would never be that. Not now someone had got to him.

When Wear reached Bleakhope, he wondered how he was going to obtain his belongings as the house was in darkness and he really did not think that Fang would be amenable to being woken by a recalcitrant member of the very people who had rebelled against his training. Suddenly headlights blazed in the darkness and he was about to run for it convinced that Coretec were after revenge for his apparent treachery when a voice he recognised screamed at him. "Get yourself into this bloody car, Wear." He grinned and followed the instruction climbing in beside Alison Sweetness. Deciding that he had unfinished business with her, and that if he did not take command now he never would he turned to her.

"Drive until I tell you to stop and then we have things to discuss." She nodded rather taken by this new, assertive Wear. The Forty-Third Glasgow Scouts enjoyed the education provided by watching Wear and Sweetness discuss things vigorously and inventively for some time before climbing back into the car and driving away.

"Lucky bastard! Jamesie muttered.

"I'm not so sure!" Snot observed perceptively.

Chapter 16

Dawn saw Mickley up early and already thinking. Having washed peremptorily and downed an ale, he found another early riser who had woken due to the pain of the bruises he had received the night before and sent him in search of the Head of Sales.

"I presume there were no, ah, difficulties last night?" Sales shook his head. His mood was not helped as the injuries he had suffered the previous night had caused his muscles to stiffen and he had not had sufficient sleep.

"No, no problems. Why?" Mickley looked at him.

"Just ensuring there were no loose ends connecting us with that little fracas. All the pub staff see the light?" Sales was a consummate liar as was demonstrated by his business success and he did not miss a beat in replying to the negative. "Hmm, well, the boys all fine and chipper? Not too bruised or battered, hmm?"

"Just the two need a bit of a rest. And you sir?" he enquired looking at Mickley's swollen nose and eyes following his meeting with the NFU chairman. Mickley glared and then resumed the mantle of bonhomie.

"Tell me, dear boy, do you think the, ah, yokels, farmers and so on, might gossip?" Sales considered.

"No, I doubt it, but there would be no harm in making a repeat call would there?"

"No, no harm at all." Sales went to search out the remains of his team and organise visits to as many farmers as possible after holding discussions with the pub staff.

Galphay was in ebullient form having thoroughly enjoyed the previous night's punch up. Naturally, he assumed that all his staff would feel the same and was enraged when it became apparent that they did not. "Idle buggers, come on, get up!" A muffled chorus of Sod Off mixed with Git made their feelings clear. Galphay went snarling to kick his Operations team awake. "Listen, you need to visit all the local farmers who were in the pub last night and make sure they remember nothing. Oh, and while your at it, make sure the pub staff remember to remember nothing as well. Now move!" He stomped off leaving Operations to try and climb to their feet. Eventually, a depleted crew walked stiffly to the pony paddock and rode off.

The mutual concern felt by both Mickley and Galphay concerning the pub staff was, in fact, wasted. The NFU chairman had briefly held an urbane chat with them that had ensured that, while baffled as to the problems that might arise if they did, were very sure that they would not tell the Police anything. He had also been up early, first to telephone all his members to ensure that they had survived the night and were not of a mind to speak to the police. He had then called the hospital to enquire as to the health of the injured Police constable and had been reassured as a caring magistrate to hear that he was still unconscious. Finally, he held a brief conversation with the investigating inspector. It never harmed to check but he was unsurprised to hear that the landlord was an obstinate so and so who refused to assist the Police in any way despite his pub having been wrecked. "Aye, it seems like some gang has moved into the area and is offering protection. I'd guess our wee boy didn't pay up."

"Interesting," the NFU chairman observed and rang off, happy that any potential problems for his members had been headed off.

Fortuitously, Coretec and Fireflow's representatives did not meet as they headed for the pub with a degree of urgency. Added to the NFU chairman's brief conversation that had already convinced those staff who spoke English to keep quiet, those whose linguistic skills were poorer were too concerned with the possibility of being deported despite their perfectly legal status, so that the cold call by Fireflow's sales staff was both confusing and unnecessary. On their departure, the staff discussed the situation amongst themselves and agreed that they had been unaware that there were Secret Police operating in the United Kingdom. With fatalistic shrugs, it was decided that it was best to continue to plead ignorance and the fact that two Fireflow staff were recognised from the previous night merely convinced the workers that dark matters involving the State were taking place and they wanted no part. Stoically, they set about trying to tidy the bar and restore it to working order.

The arrival of Coretec's depleted Operations team brought this approach to an abrupt end. To be fair to the Pub staff, they put up considerably more resistance than their employer to the coercive techniques applied by Coretec but the end result was the same. The Head of Operations was breathing hard as he waved a hand at his stick-wielding henchmen. "Look, all we want..." He was interrupted by a scornful, if pained laugh from the floor from an English speaking worker. "As I was saying, we just want to make sure we understand one another and that you remember to forget anything you saw last night." He sighed as he was roundly cursed in various Slavic tongues. Following ten seconds of stick wielding, he finally had his agreement and the Coretec contingent left the Pub.

Unfortunately, when the Police appeared dragging the Publican with them, the Pub staff had decided that attack was the best form of defence. From the car park, the Inspector radioed for assistance from uniform. "Tango five to Tango, back up to the Sluggish Trout! Fast! What the bloody hell – no, not you! Just send back up." He ducked behind the car as a bottle flung from the kitchen just missed him. His sergeant, bleeding profusely from a scalp wound was swearing in a monotone. "What the hell have we found here?" the Inspector demanded.

"Bastards, ruined my new shirt. This'll never wash out!"

"Sergeant! Who are these people?"

"Foreign bastards! No Europeans anyway!" The sergeant's ignorance of ethnic backgrounds led to a rapid escalation in the situation.

The rapidly growing drama at the pub created a clear field for Coretec and Fireflow as they set about tying up any loose ends. The by now terrified Pub staff stared in horror as first the Police Armed Response Unit, then an Anti Terrorist Squad from the Army rapidly took up positions following the Police Inspector radioing in that the incident involved non Europeans who over reacted dramatically to simple questioning. The Publican found himself apparently berated by his staff who pushed him out the back door where he was subdued and processed with despatch. Unaware that he was meant to be telling the authorities that his staff was hard working and law abiding and wished to resign and go home, the army interrogators rapidly gained a garbled tale of demands to be returned home. The senior Intelligence officer regarded the whimpering figure of the landlord. "Better check his story again, sergeant." He ignored the screams from the Publican as he wrote up his notes. Finally, he looked severely at the unfortunate. "Look, international terrorism is bloody unpleasant. We need answers fast so the end justifies the means. In our world there are no individual rights, the government agrees so, either you tell us what we need or…" He let the statement hang until the Publican started talking.

The Head of Fireflow Sales looked up as an army helicopter clattered low overhead scaring his pony. "What are they up to?" His colleagues were unable to supply an answer as the machine banked steeply to land just out of sight of the pub. "Right, sure we got all the farmers names from that harridan in the shop?" His men nodded. "Right, we'll start with Hard Hills and then go to Hungry Knowe." Coretec had also visited the local shop for information and a chat as to who regularly attended the pub. By now, the shopkeeper and his wife were keen to try anything rather than suffer any further conversations. As the junior Operations team member emptied the shelves over the counter with his stick, the shopkeeper added a further dimension to the suffering of the district. "For God's sake, what do you want? Money? Just stop, please." The Head of Operations dropped him and looked at him carefully.

"Not money, no. But food would be useful." While Coretec were making arrangements for regular deliveries of provisions, Fireflow were reaching a similar agreement with Archie at Hard Hills. Ever a realist, Archie cursed the fact that he did not have his gun with him and that the dogs were in an outbuilding. As usual, the clicking of lighters acted as a background to the urbane tones of the Head of Sales. Archie agreed that fire was an ever present danger on farms and could wreak havoc in minutes. Ever reasonable, the Fireflow pitch offered complete assurance that such an unpleasant fate would never occur to Archie, provided he was willing to provide a few cattle to the Head of Sales. A hard man himself, Archie fully understood the message as a small outbuilding spontaneously combusted,

As Coretec clattered down the track towards Bare Lee, they remarked on the column of smoke rising to the south. "Wonder what's happening there?"

"Dunno. Still, nothing to do with us." Bare Lee heard the telephone ringing as he stared at the riders trotting into his fold yard. While he was discussing the previous evening's events and his suddenly fading memories of them, Archie cut the connection on his telephone just before Fireflow pulled down the telephone wires as they drove their new cattle out the road end. If Bare Lee was out in the fields, he'd try Hard Hills. The inert state of his telephone told him everything he needed to know. With a sigh, he checked that the remains of the outbuilding were sufficiently soaked so as not to re-ignite and headed for his tractor.

The crow, floating over the landscape searching for its next meal, viewed the considerable human activity occurring with vague interest. Two separate lots of horsemen with cattle were moving across the country in different directions, an old, grey Ferguson tractor was hurtling along the road and then the bird swerved violently as it spotted obvious men with guns around the village and the sound of gunshots reached it on the breeze. Deciding that there would be safer pickings elsewhere, the crow flapped hard away to the north.

The Pub staff lay behind the stainless steel ovens and Bain Maries in the kitchen and screamed questions at one another regarding who the hell was attacking them now. Finally, and fatally, a Hungarian remembered his grandfather's tales of the uprising and crawled in search of some empty bottles while shouting for others to find rags and any flammable liquids. The Inspector, long supplanted from his control of the situation regarded the troops' commander with incredulity. "Are you sure they're Al Quieda? I thought they were illegal workers! At worst some sort of drugs ring!"

"Well, the publican Johnny tells us that they're demanding safe conduct home and something about hostages, and you know what the world is like these days. Best thing would be if they fought back, eliminate the problem, so to speak." The inspector goggled.

"That's murder!"

"Well, we'll give them a last chance to surrender and then I'll let the boys loose." His radio receiver crackled as one of the watching snipers informed him that there was activity in the kitchen. They turned to watch just as the first Molotov Cocktail sailed in a flaming arc out the window to unerringly smash through the windscreen of the Inspector's car turning it into a blazing wreck in seconds. The first rounds cracked across the car park as the soldiers reacted to the threat and the pub staff roared defiance and hurled more petrol bombs.

Fang regarded Galphay's messenger with loathing. "Explain what you mean by 'benefit in kind'?" he demanded.

"Well, do we get additional points for expanding our herd? If people choose to make us presents? Not stolen or anything."

"I suppose so. But why would they want to give you lot cattle?" The herald shrugged.

"No idea, but four have already. Maybe they're just friendly and want us to win. We'd a good chat with them last night!" Fang finally agreed that, unlikely as such a scenario seemed, it was within the rules of the exercise. A nearly identical discussion shortly thereafter with Fireflow sent Fang in search of the girls and whisky. "The bastards are up to something," he muttered darkly and the girls had to agree.

"And he was polite?" queried Alice.

"That's what really worries me! They're never polite, not like the other lunatics!" Fang's views on the trainees had crystallised since his escape from the vengeful Coretec. He now treated them with a wary disdain and ensured he never turned his back. "We need to find out what has been happening. Time for a visit to the pub!" The girls agreed and they set off for a pleasant walk in the evening sunshine. As they went, Fang remarked that they still seemed to burn stubble in the area despite the rules prohibiting such a practice. Certainly, three separate columns of smoke could be seen rising on the still air.

As they neared the pub, they noticed the presence of a large number of Police vehicles and several Range Rovers. "What has happened?" Sonya wondered. Before the others could pontificate, an armed policeman emerged from the bushes and stopped them going any further.

"There's an incident at the pub but it is under control. I'm sorry, you can't go any further!"

"Damn!" Fang cursed. "We won't get a drink tonight!" The policeman laughed nastily.

"Judging by what is going on, you won't get a drink there ever again!" The trio looked at each other and then headed for the village shop. They stopped once when the unmistakeable sound of machine gun fire punctuated by single shots smashed the silence. They speeded up and soon were pushing open the door of the shop. They were greeted by the shopkeeper's wife, who uttered a shriek and vanished in to the back of the shop. "Odd," Fang remarked just before the shopkeeper burst into the room clutching a shotgun. "We only called in to buy a few things!" Fang observed as Alice and Sonya rapidly stepped behind him.

"Oh, it's you!" The shopkeeper lowered his weapon. "I thought those bastards had come back!"

"Ah, well, we're not. Those bastards, I mean. What the hell has been going on?" Fang enquired.

"Some heavy bastards rode up, and..."

"You mean on motor bikes?"

"No, horses and then, hang on you won't say anything to the Police will you?" An appalled Fang readily assured him he would not and heard the tales of the visitations the shop had suffered. "And that was after last night in the pub! Never seen anything like it!"

"You'd better explain," Fang ordered in a resigned voice.

When they finally left the shop, Fang was drinking straight from the bottle of whisky he had purchased. "Dear Christ! What will they do next?"

"Something horrible!" prophesised Alice and Sonya nodded her head in agreement. Just then, two journalists stepped out of a car and into their path.

"What the hell do you want!" Fang snarled defensively.

"Local colour!" one journalist replied. "What does the village think of a terrorist cell in its midst? Did you ever speak to them or anything? Has your life been ruined by this?" Fang looked at him in amazement.

"All I can say is that there seems to be some incident at the pub and we heard gunshots, other than that, I haven't a clue!" The journalists watched them go.

"Bloody Police have got to them already!" His silent colleague shrugged and they both turned towards the pub as more shots were heard. Spent pellets pattered around them and a louder explosion thumped their ears. "Odd place this, cattle rustling, terrorist cells, a better level of Omerta than the mafia can impose! Never known anything like it!"

As they walked back up the drive in the gloaming, the sound of hoof beats grew louder and they quietly stepped into the shadows and watched Fireflow jingle passed and out of sight. Mutely shaking his head, Fang set off homewards once more. When they were out of earshot, several scouts rose from the vegetation. "They seem awfie' scared."

"Aye, weel, that was the wan that they others were after chasing, but." Soon, they reverted to their favourite topic since observing the Wear Sweetness discussion, female figures, and lost interest in the Fang contingent other than Alice and Sonya's figures. They headed back to the camp to report their observations to the students and tell the minister a fanciful tale of bird watching. They stopped when a lurid flash lit the sky over the village followed a couple of seconds later by a tremendous blast. A siren wailed a lonely message and alarms sounded faintly. The Pub staff's last stand had finally ended.

Chapter 17

The passing of the Fireflow riders witnessed by Fang and the girls was the first indication of a refinement of the new tactics of intimidation being carried out by both sides. It seemed a sensible development based on sound business tactics of capturing the existing customers of rivals to grow one's own client base. Accordingly, having viewed the success of a single day's efforts by the Sales team, Mickley had been contemplating how best to improve the return on effort and to use all his staff. The arrival of several scouts who still persisted in supporting Fireflow against Coretec, provided him with the insight he required to move matters forward. Mickley listened to the scouts report with interest. "So, those scoundrels are preying on farmers and demanding livestock with menaces?"

"Eh?" The scouts did not understand Mickley's rhetoric.

"Well, are they carrying out a protection racket?"

"Ah didnae see much protection, but..." stated Jamesie.

"Hmm, what did you see, precisely?" Jamesie considered the question.

"Well, they welly the farmer wi' sticks, and then they get cattle and ride aff."

"Ah, well, I suppose they would. Hardly subtle, hmm?" The scouts shrugged en masse, it seemed no less subtle than burning buildings but they refrained from saying so. After providing the scouts with some food obtained from the village shop, Mickley called his Heads of Department for a discussion on tactics. While they huddled together, the scouts drifted away muttering darkly.

"He disnae seem interested in giving yon lot a good kicking," Jamesie remarked and the others agreed. They returned to their camp busily discussing ways in which to incite more direct action from Fireflow against Coretec

Several unfortunate farmers named by the scouts received a visit from Fireflow that night and had the error of relying on

Coretec for protection explained to them in simple terms. In each case, the result was the same, cattle were driven off while behind them a haystack or building burned. The farmers' plight was worsened by the total collapse of the telephone network and the knowledge that the Police viewed the assault on their local officer as part of the terrorist activity they had uncovered. None were foolish enough to suggest that they had been involved in any fashion and the frenzied efforts of the security forces and Police to make some sense of the events at the Sluggish Trout underlined the benefit of admitting to nothing. The news that the publican had been detained indefinitely for further questioning confirmed the popular view that continuing silence was best.

In addition to hindering the Authorities investigations, the refusal to admit to any knowledge of events or the protagonists by the local community, left the Press in the unfamiliar position of having no one to question as to how they felt. Attempts to interview Constable Findlay had merely resulted in phone calls to their editors threatening a gagging order and it soon became hard to justify the cost of expense accounts, helicopters and in depth interviews with the Evergreen Club from Gourock who merely expressed dismay that their favourite place for afternoon tea had been closed indefinitely and, more immediately, that there were no public conveniences open in the area. Watching various desperate elderly gentlemen head for the bushes beside the road, ignoring the attempts by the Police present to stop them, did not seem likely to provide the sort of story that would pacify the cost accountants back at their respective headquarters. Soon, the predilection of a minor politician to charge the hire of his mistress' costumes on parliamentary expenses provided the excuse the news teams required to leave. As the Police were fully occupied with trying to establish if they had eradicated what they believed was a terrorist cell, the field was now wide open for Coretec and Fireflow to further develop their feud.

While Archie continued to attempt to rally his farming colleagues to present a united front against the riders from Coretec and Fireflow, the demoralised state of the agricultural community rendered his attempts futile. "Look, Archie," Bare Lees informed him, "they've given me a good beating, taken half my herd and torched two buildings. Me? I'm just going to sit it out. No offence, but I'm not getting involved. Anyway, get noticed and the Police either shoot you or take you away. Sorry."

Archie grunted with disappointment and rumbled off perched on his tractor while his dogs ran behind. The tale was too familiar to cause him any surprise although he was disappointed at how supine his neighbours were proving. He cheered himself by driving at some Fireflow riders he met on the road and only reluctantly whistled his dogs away as they snapped and snarled at the rear legs of the horses. Ignoring the angry yells and threats of retribution he continued on his way.

The situation also had a negative effect on tourism with those visitors not put off with the news of a major, if undisclosed terrorist incident, finding the locals taciturn to the point of rudeness. While some merely put the situation down to natural reticence, the majority rapidly concluded they could spend their money elsewhere and at least appear to have their presence welcomed. This in turn added to the frustration and anger of the local community who relied heavily on the money of visitors to help them survive. The first stirrings of resistance, other than Archie's efforts, and he had always been known for enjoying a fight more than work or drink, occurred amongst the females in the community. The Women's Guild at their monthly meeting at the church blithely ignored their agenda and their guest speaker who had been invited to lecture on a visit to the Holy Land, to debate the situation.

"Madam Chairman, I move that we devote the evening to debating whit to dae about those bastards." The Chairwoman's response was drowned out by screams and yells of agreement from the floor. Looking at her membership, the Chairwoman could not help noting with pride that they were a formidable bunch. She permitted the change to the meeting with good grace and opened the floor to suggestions. With organisational skills honed by years of organising bring and buy stalls, famine relief and bringing up families, the Guild rapidly came up with plans for resistance that would not attract the notice of the Police, Security Service or their husbands. It would take several days to put their intentions into action, but the initial discussions were encouraging. "Now, you're sure about this, Deirdre?"

"Oh aye, no problem."

"And you Jeannie. You've got all the equipment you need?" Jeanie agreed that she had. After going over the plan once more, the meeting ushered up a brief prayer for divine support and broke up after swearing each other to silence.

Findlay was finely discharged from hospital on indefinite sick leave and with absolutely no memory of what had happened on the fateful evening. He had a confused memory of poachers eluding him and an intention to follow up on some livestock thefts, but other than that, he met only swirling confusion when he tried to recall the events that had led to his hospital stay. Despite the best efforts of the medical fraternity and his colleagues in CID, he could provide no information. It had been established that he had received a call from the Sluggish Trout, but what he had found and what had happened thereafter was unknown to the Authorities. Rather than regarding Findlay as a hero who had obviously attempted to take on a terrorist cell single handed, his senior officers were busily attempting to place the blame for the whole incident on him to cover up their own failings to identify any risk existing in their area. The only man who tried to help Findlay was the Inspector, who although he did not like Findlay professionally, having a deep distrust of his background, regarded him as honest and hardworking. Anyway, the poor bugger was being hung out to dry by the upper echelons and those well-dressed southerners up from London. The Inspector distrusted them all and naturally sided with the man on the ground even if he was an overqualified oddity.

Once he had driven Findlay home from the hospital, the Inspector tried to make sure that he was in a fit state to look after himself and had enough food in the house. Findlay's responses had shocked him. "Help? Here? No sir, most unlikely, I'm seen as the law and to be kept at arms length."

"Well, surely a neighbour will call in and check you are all right?" Findlay shook his head and winced.

"The neighbours hate me I'm afraid. Mrs Dodds has never forgiven me for arresting her son for poaching, and the Turnbulls blame me for his losing his licence."

"Ah." The Inspector regarded him with interest. "And?" he finally enquired.

"Well, I gave the boy an official warning, or pretended to rather than give him a criminal record but she is convinced I've blighted his future. But I'd nothing to do with Traffic pulling over the Turnbulls after their Golden wedding." The Inspector shook his head.

"Well, maybe you need to lighten up or try harder or something." Findlay sighed but did not bother to respond. Having checked the fridge and freezer, the Inspector regarded Findlay worriedly.

"Look, I'll get you some food from the shop. You'll starve otherwise." On his return, the Inspector regarded Findlay with more sympathy. "Unfriendly lot in this village," he observed and Findlay nodded carefully.

"They don't like the Police, they're terrified of someone despite the terrorists having been taken care of! What the hell is going on? I've never had a shop keeper make the sign of the evil eye at me before!" Findlay laughed,

"Yes, she's a bit odd but it's a change from her gossiping!" After a few minutes of desultory chat, the Inspector left promising to look in the next day.

It should have surprised neither Fireflow nor Coretec when their rivalry escalated into actual violence. With both having every possible rider out trying to gain the greatest number of cattle and 'clients', a clash was inevitable. Probably the keenest in pushing the Fireflow message, were the former hostages who were aware that they were still regarded with suspicion by their new colleagues. Accordingly, they were constantly in the saddle scouring for any signs of back sliding amongst their client farmers. The light from a burning barn lit by them, attracted in several Coretec employees and the sight of each other was sufficient to lead to blows. A brief fist fight broke out that turned ugly with the use of staves by the outnumbered Fireflow henchmen. The farmer watched the now horse borne skirmish whirl out of his yard to the clatter of hooves, wood on wood and loud cursing and swearing.

"At least they forgot to take more cattle," he observed bitterly to his wife.

"I think I saw one knocked out the saddle," she replied grimly. The farmer's face brightened and he whistled up his skulking dog.

"Let's go and see," he informed her. Soon further screams echoed in the night as the farmer and his dog provided aid to the fallen Coretec salesman. The approach of the farmer's spouse clutching garden shears helped him to his feet despite his injuries and he blundered away into the dark with the collie snapping and snarling at his heels. Several scouts watched with interest as a moaning figure staggered out the dark and passed their hiding place.

"Had a bit o' a shoeing," one observed as the figure vanished once more into the gloom and only the pained sounds remained.

The latest defeat to Fireflow heralded by the return of the battered group minus a rider and his mount, hit Coretec, and particularly Galphay, hard.

"What the hell happened to you?" he demanded. They explained that they had seen a farm building burning, gone to investigate seeing it was one of 'their' farms, and been jumped by a superior force from Fireflow wielding staves. In the resultant fight they had been forced to retreat.

"And I bet they took cattle as well," added the spokesman gloomily. Galphay was explaining the pathetic nature of their efforts and their total lack of that essential drive that made a Coretec employee, when he was interrupted by the painful return of the previously unnoticed missing salesman.

"You bastards!" he announced as he limped torn and bleeding into the firelight. The assembled throng gazed at him in wonder. Initially the Fireflow converts had done a good job on him but the farmer had surpassed them in his efforts and the dog had taken the opportunity to show what a collie could achieve to the extreme. Despite all this, it was the farmer's wife and her shears that had made the most impression on the sufferer's mind and he uselessly babbled about gelding and shears when questioned so that his colleagues eyed him with horror. He was finally led away still totally preoccupied by the nightmare of what might have befallen him. Galphay tried to enthuse and stiffen his followers to take the fight to Fireflow but the damage had been done. They rode out no more that night allowing Fireflow free access to all the farms that they could reach. Instead, Coretec spent a wakeful night as their injured colleague's exhausted sleep was enlivened by screaming nightmares.

Alice carefully carried two mugs of coffee up the uneven stairs of Bleakhope tower with the aid of a head torch. Fang was exactly where she had left him, on the roof platform gazing morosely over the countryside. "Here, mug of coffee." Alice informed him.

"They're burning half the countryside, look." Fang did not seem to have heard her.

"Ian, you can't do anything tonight. Drink your coffee and let's go to bed. You'll suss out what to do by morning." Fang shook his head unseen in the dark.

"Alice, if I try to speak to them, they try and kill me! If I do nothing, then the Police will blame us! God knows why it has taken them so long to come and demand information on the crowd of lunatics I brought in and turned loose on the district!" Alice placed the mugs on the battlement and shook his arm roughly.

"Look, they're only playing at being reivers, your lot were for centuries. You'll work out what to do! Now come on, coffee and bed." Sighing, Fang did as he was instructed but as he fell asleep he could see the flare of burning farms in his mind's eye and hear the knock of the Police at his door.

The next morning, Fang had rediscovered his resolve and rode out at first light to visit the two camps. It was obviously essential that he rein in both Coretec and Fireflow. The rapidly expanding list of their offences against society were simply too much and he was determined to regain control. Sadly, this bullish approach did not last. He was found gazing open-mouthed at the vast herd of cattle that surrounded the Fireflow camp. Somehow, he regained his speech when they took him to see Mickley. "Must be well ahead on points by now," Mickley informed him cheerfully.

"Where the fucking hell did you find them?" Fang demanded viciously. Mickley raised an eyebrow, an affectation that fared badly in view of his rapidly growing beard and crumpled attire.

"Oh, we didn't find them, they were given to us." Fang somehow controlled himself.

"For the last time, this has got to stop. If it doesn't" he announced with prophetic accuracy, "you will suffer!" Mickley laughed.

"I'll bear that in mind. Now, when can we expect more food?" Fang strode back to his pony, mounted and rode off without a word.

His visit to Coretec was equally fruitless and just as disturbing. To his fevered eye, the herd of cattle seemed no smaller than that possessed by Fireflow. Also, the sight of the farmer's revenge wrapped in various home-made bandages as he limped slowly past talking to himself was distinctly unnerving. Coretec were strangely sullen but lacked their usual arrogant hint of latent violence. Again, Fang tried to impress on them the need to revert to law abiding participation in a training exercise, but they were obdurate in their refusal to listen. Instead, Fang was subjected to a litany of complaints from Galphay as to the misdemeanours of Fireflow and the need to humble them in response. Eventually, Fang gave up and rode away. He carefully considered what he had seen and realised with a frisson of horror that both parties had lost their grip on reality and time. It was if he had stumbled on an earlier, more brutal age where revenge overrode every other consideration and the end justified the means. On returning to Bleakhope, Sonya and Alice waited for him to speak. His words struck a chill in them both. "They want only to shake loose the border," he quoted and retired to the top of the tower once more.

Chapter 18

Wear pulled the door shut behind him and clutching a bundle of newspapers, wandered into the bedroom and sat down next to Alison Sweetness who was half hidden under the covers. "Well?" she enquired.

"No mention of anything on the front pages," Wear replied morosely. She sat up and stared at him.

"There must be, look at what the bastards did before we left!" Wear shrugged.

"You'd think that two well-known companies were never involved in a mass brawl or that they had taken to assaulting children or stealing cattle. I mean, you'd expect it all over the papers!" Sweetness glared at him.

"Stop being so pathetic. Question is, why is there no story about them? They haven't got that sort of clout." Wear looked at her.

"You never know, but I doubt it. Maybe something more interesting displaced it."

"Christ!" Sweetness exploded. "What, some bloody politician dressing his tart up at public expense? Nah!" She sat silent for a moment then grinned. "D'you want me to dress up as Cat Woman or Nell Gwinn?" Wear considered the idea with a smirk. "Look like that and I'll dress as Super Nanny," she informed him and mistook his inadvertent squirm of distaste as pleasure. "You kinky little bastard! Well, if you're a good boy all day we'll have to see!"

"No, no!" Wear hastened to try and correct her but she merely smiled and picked up a paper to scan it.

Fifteen minutes later, Sweetness climbed out of bed and went to make some coffee. Wear watched her leave the room with faint trepidation. Although he found her exciting and far more fun than he had ever imagined, he was wary of her sudden enthusiasms and being treated to an evening of being ordered about did not strike him as even faintly approaching anything other than cringe inducing. She wandered back into the room carrying two mugs and her mobile and handed him a coffee before climbing under the covers once more. "Who are you planning on phoning?" Wear wondered.

"Well, let's face it, those bastards have screwed our careers and the only way I see of ensuring no mud sticks, is to be seen as the sane ones who were fired for being whistle blowers!"

"Eh?

They fired us and we haven't blown any whistles that I've heard!" Sweetness looked at him. "Are you being deliberately naughty, darling?"

Wear decided against glaring at her in case it encouraged her.

"No, I just can't see how we can twist things to make us look good while dropping those bastards right in it!" Sweetness smiled.

"Drink your coffee and I'll tell you!" He did as he was told and Sweetness enlightened him. When she had finished, Wear nodded.

"It could work, but you know how they twist everything! Still, we've nothing to lose, let's give it a go!"

Wear had a shower while Sweetness made several calls and finally came to inform him of how she had got on. "Well, we're having lunch out today. I got one interested but we'll see if he comes up to scratch." Wear stepped out of the shower and grabbed a towel.

"Why wouldn't he? I mean it seems as good a story as any, so where would there be a problem?" Sweetness shook her head.

"I dunno. He said there had been a nearly story but no one would talk and then the Security Services came over all heavy and they were forced to drop it. If we get him interested he'll publish despite everything, if we don't then we're screwed!" Wear regarded her with a frown.

"Sounds unlikely, threats from the Security Services! What did the others have to say?"

"Well, that was the interesting thing! They were all intrigued with the idea that I might have a major scandal for them but as soon as I said where the scandal had taken place, they lost interest. Like yesterday." Wear shook his head.

"Don't see how that helps us, I mean if there is only one interested, I mean, where does that leave us?" Sweetness contrived to look smug.

"Well, lover, all the responsible ones basically corroborated each other and made it plain there was some sort of a story but they couldn't publish it and the only one willing to talk was from the Guardian!"

"So?" This time Sweetness actually giggled with pleasure.

"He's far more likely to publish if the rest won't and so is his editor. They're mad on Press Freedom and hate being told what they can and cannot write by the Establishment. Interest him and we're home and published!"

The lunch meeting had been arranged for the latest trendy restaurant in the city where the décor was superb, every one who was anyone liked to come to be insulted by the celebrity chef, an appallingly rude northerner who affected to despise all Londoners and the food was average at best. The prices were not and Wear morosely tried to remember the exact state of his bank balance as they waited for their guest to appear. Sweetness sat and enjoyed the whirl of self-important humanity as it wandered in to be insulted and fleeced in equal measure. A supercilious barman sighed when they ordered soda and lime.

"Saving for the meal are we?" he enquired. Wear ignored the comment but Sweetness did not.

"Listen, you little gimp, if I want to drink soda water that's my business. Your business is to serve me and pretend to enjoy the experience. Clear?" The barman flounced off and Wear sighed.

"Now he'll probably spit in our drinks!" he observed.

"Nah, he'll avoid us and make us wait so it doesn't seem like we are spinning our drinks out. Anyway, he's the monkey not the organ grinder." Wear smiled despite himself.

"And when our guest arrives?"

"Oh. They'll be all over him and forget that they don't like us. It pays to be nice to journalists, you never know when one is acting food critic for the week or something."

They were both surprised when the chef appeared swaggering through the crowd in his whites and failing to avoid contact with anyone so that his progress was marked by a series of minor collisions as he barged through gaps rather than easing his way.

"Eeeh, which of you upset my barman? He's weeping in the kitchen, like!" Sweetness glared at him.

"If you mean who explained he was an unpleasant little shit with no manners, that'll be me. Why?" The chef glared.

"Way aye! You're the bitch I want a woourd with!" Wear burst into fits of giggles so that they both turned furious gazes on him.

"Come on, Brian!" He said and started laughing again. The angry look on Sweetness' face changed to one of confusion while the chef stared at Wear. Wear managed to stop laughing again. "I don't know what you call yourself here, but you never had as strong a Geordie accent as that when were growing up! What an act!" He burst into laughter again and the chef sat down and grinned.

"Aye, well, they love it down here. Give them what they think we are like and add a bit of rudeness and belligerence? Every table covered three times over. Speak normally and treat people well? Bailiffs are in by the end of the week. What are you up to anyway and you haven't introduced your friend." Wear explained that they had arranged a meeting with a journalist over lunch and who Sweetness was. Despite the outbreak of pleasantries she was still suspicious.

"What about your barman?"

"He'll enjoy the drama when I kick his arse for being rude to friends. In the meantime, he can flounce to his friends. I'll sort a table for you. My treat." He vanished and Wear burst out laughing again.

"What?" Sweetness snapped.

"Just he used to be teased for speaking posh and now look at him! Brilliant, and this looks like our guest."

While the introductions were made and a red eyed barman took their orders politely and with alacrity, Wear studied the journalist. He was rather disappointed to see that Detchant Middleton was a well-groomed man wearing a sober grey suit and muted tie. When offered a drink he requested a fruit juice. Wear was faintly disappointed at this healthy approach and wondered what had happened to the hard drinking journalists of popular repute.

"I need to work this afternoon and drink doesn't help me meet deadlines or write very well. Same way as I will just have a light lunch if you don't mind. I'll fall asleep otherwise." Middleton felt the need to explain. Wear stifled a yawn. Somehow he didn't feel illegal substances played any part in the bloke's life either. He hoped he devoted his time to puritanical thoughts and attacking capitalists. They ordered carefully, Middleton in keeping with his austere approach to life, Sweetness and Wear in deference to their financial position.

"Right, very pleasant," the journalist announced dead panned when they finished eating. "Explain how you feel that you have a worthwhile story for me." He held up a hand as Sweetness opened her mouth to respond. "I'll need to corroborate everything by the way."

"Of course. We'd hope for nothing less!" Wear interjected hastily when he saw the look on Sweetness' face. "Look, are you interested in hearing how two major companies are assaulting children, stealing cattle, and fighting with one another in country pubs while encouraged by their respective MDs?"

"Depends on who they are and how truthful your account is." Sweetness had regained her composure.

"Well, if I explain that we were tasked by our individual MDs to find alternative training following an article..." Again she was brusquely interrupted.

"Yes, yes, I read it. Poor journalism! Nothing of interest there." Wear kicked Sweetness under the table.

"Look." He paused as Sweetness opened her capacious handbag hoping she was not going to produce a cosh to use on their guest.

"Here, my briefing and a copy of his, together with copies of what the training company sent." The journalist took them without speaking and, folding them carefully, placed them in his jacket pocket.

"And?" he prompted.

"Well, do the names Coretec and Fireflow mean anything to you?" Middleton nodded, poker-faced. "Right, well." Wear looked to Sweetness for support. She did not disappoint.

"I presume you have a Dictaphone recording as I doubt your memory is very good," she informed the journalist. He smiled and nodded. "Right, this is what has happened so far." She launched into a precise description of the events at Reiver Management Training.

When Sweetness finally stopped talking, Middleton lent back in his chair. A waiter appeared instantly with coffee and they waited until he had gone.

"Interesting," the journalist observed. "Can you give me names of people who can corroborate all this?" Sweetness nodded.

"I made a list of witnesses and participants who can confirm what we have told you. I'm sure they've been up to further mischief since we left, but I can't confirm that."

"Oh, I will, believe me. Now, why did you come to me?" Wear decided to be honest.

"Well, we've both lost our jobs and we feel we've been stiffed by our employers so this is partly revenge!"

"Only partly?"

"Well, if you do your job well enough, totally. All we want is it made plain that our work had nothing to do with how those lunatics chose to behave. Think of us as whistle blowers!" The journalist shrugged.

"Depends what I find out as to how I treat you when I publish. I mean. If you encouraged all this and are trying to dodge the blame, then I'll include you in the mess. If you didn't then your name will be in shining lights. Now, why the hell was a gagging order put on any stories out of the area?" They both shook their head, plainly unaware of any such event. "Fair enough, well, I'll get started and see what I can find. Be good to nail those bastards to the wall!" He stood up and left. Wear looked at Sweetness.

"Well?"

"What a prick!" she giggled. "Just the man to prove what they've been up to. I'm sorry though, I don't feel like being Super Nanny, but Cat Woman feels like celebrating!" Their mood was further helped when their attempts to pay for the meal was rebuffed.

"No way! Look, ring and book a table one evening and we can have a good chat." They shook hands with the now clearly spoken chef and left.

Back at the Guardian, Middleton pitched his story hard. "Look, there is obviously Police corruption or they would have stopped this nonsense straight off rather than gagging the press. Second, you know there have been stories as to both companies business approach although no one has ever spoken out and that's suspicious and lastly, I can smell a good story!" The editor tapped his keyboard meditatively.

"All right, Detchant, go and see if you can prove any of this. Keep it quiet so if there is a story we don't alert the rest and spoil it and make sure the authorities don't get a whiff you are looking in the area. Once we publish it's hard to put the cork back in the bottle. Best defence really." An hour later, the journalist was driving North and planning who to approach first. Nothing excited him more than humbling big business and showing up their failings except, he admitted to himself, the opportunity to make the authorities look corrupt or inefficient. Something convinced him that there was an interesting tale just waiting to be uncovered.

An exhausted and severely scratched Wear muttered a curse when the phone rang and he reached over a supine Sweetness still clad in the tattered lycra remnants of her costume. "Yes?" He listened with growing interest and then sat up. "Say that again, please." Sweetness swore quietly. "Excellent, well if we can be of any further help, just ring or email us. You've got our contact details. Good luck!" He put the phone down with a smirk. "That was our dining companion, dear Detchant is heading North notebook in hand!" Sweetness looked at him.

"Miaow!" she announced and dragged her nails across his chest.

Chapter 19

Fang cursed when he heard the knock at the door. He was in no mood to deal with passing strangers seeking directions or travellers offering to tarmac his drive for cash. He had spent the previous night until two in the morning up on the tower although for once there had been no obvious fires to signal that Coretec and Fireflow were about their business. He had finally given up his lonely vigil and retired to bed to lie awake and worry what the wretched trainees were up to unseen. Accordingly, he did not look with favour at the figure who stood on his doorstep. "Yes?"

"Ah. Good morning, are you Ian Fang?"

"Yes, and I'm not buying. Goodbye." Fang started to shut the door when he stopped on hearing the words.

"Quite, I'm Detchant Middleton from the Guardian. I wondered if..." Middleton stepped down from the doorstep when Fang reappeared suddenly.

"Who did you say you were?" Fang snarled, obeying the dictum that attack is the best form of defence.

"Detchant Middleton, from the Guardian." Fang smiled unpleasantly.

"Very well, and why are you door stepping me, Mr Middleton?" Middleton gulped despite his strongly held views on the land owning classes.

"Well, I hoped that you might be able to provide me with your side of the story?" He paused deliberately but Fang skirted round the opening gambit with ease.

"Story? No story here. I told your colleagues from another red top that I was totally unaware of what had been happening in the village. I know the pub blew up, but that's all. Better ask around there. Gossipy types." Middleton gazed in wonder at this obvious scion of the gentry. His arrogance was obviously bred in the bone and, despite himself, Middleton admitted, slightly scary.

Particularly as Fang was so young and looked fit and hard despite, or perhaps because of his torn jeans and unshaven stubble.

"That's not the story I was talking about..." Middleton tried to regain the initiative but Fang was up to the attempt.

"Well, I can't help you if you're confused can I? I suggest you go to the village and see what you can grub up. Good day to you." This time the door shut with finality leaving Middleton to return cursing to his car.

Once he was sure that Middleton had gone, Fang fled in search of Alice. Having found her in the bath, he started to rant. "I knew it! I bloody knew it. Now what the hell are we going to do? Bloody press on the doorstep, next thing it will be the Police and then a bunch of lawyers! "Alice raised a shapely leg out of the water and extended it, appearing to eye her limb critically.

"Sorry, darling, what were you saying?" Fang goggled at her and swore.

"I'm talking about bloody nemesis!" he bellowed.

"How exciting. You can dry my back and tell me about it." She stood up and stepped dripping onto the floor in front of him. Mutely he accepted the towel she offered him and did as he was told. Alice hummed gently as Fang dried her all the while recounting his brief meeting with Middleton. She did not let him know she had heard the whole discussion through the open window over the front door. When Fang finally ended his tale she turned to face him and smiled. "No problem, I can see how to deal with this." Fang gave a half-hearted smile in response.

"How?" Alice looked him up and down languidly.

"Jump in the bath and then I'll explain. I'm off to dress."

"Alice, come on!" He found she had gone and morosely did as he was told.

Bathed and having shaved, Fang wandered to their bedroom to dress to find to his amazement, Alice lying on the bedcover wearing stockings and a Basque. She eyed him critically. "You're overdressed," she remarked looking meaningfully at the towel around his waist.

"Alice, we need to talk, not enjoy ourselves!" She didn't answer, merely twitched his towel free. Several minutes later, Alice momentarily stopped driving Fang out of his mind with her antics.

"Now, the gentlemen of the press!" she announced.

"Stop babbling, for God's sake" Alice smiled gently and hummed, rocking gently to and fro before abruptly stopping again.

"The press," she announced. Fang gave up. "

The press. What do we do about them?"

"Well," she squirmed and so did Fang. "I can sort them out but there is one thing stopping me! Down to you really." Fang gazed at her.

"Come on Alice!" She decided to pretend that he meant her to explain further about how to deal with the press.

"Well, it's quite simple, I like here, I like you and I'd like to be Lady Fang." She gave a little squirm of encouragement.

"All right, please marry me but later!" Fang yelled. Alice resumed her activities with renewed vigour. Finally, an exhausted Fang looked down at her smiling face. "Fine, we'll marry, but you won't benefit much when I'm locked up!"

"No one will arrest my husband!" she assured him with finality. "Now, you need to go down to the village, find that reporter and invite him to dinner. I'll sort him."

Sonya had also overheard the conversation between Middleton and Fang and the subsequent noises from upstairs that suggested that they were not in need of her company or opinions. She decided to go for a walk and wandered off down the drive. A sudden scream made her turn and she saw an obviously naked Alice waving furiously out of an open window. "We're getting married!" Sonya smiled and gave a thumbs up.

"Damn," she muttered under her breath. "Brilliant! I'll see you later!" she called and set off again. Sonya was deeply disappointed. Despite the problems caused by the course participants, she had thoroughly enjoyed sharing a house with Fang and Alice. She did not miss the city at all and she had hoped that the whole thing would continue indefinitely. Now, despite being pleased for the two of them, she was pretty sure that their long-term plans as a married couple would not involve her living with them. She sniffed once or twice but kept on walking. It was always the same, she thought mournfully. Every time things seemed to be going well, something came and spoiled them. She blew her nose and walked on, soon reaching the village and, despite herself, stopped to look at the scene taking place on the doorstep of the Police House.

Findlay had totally misunderstood Detchant Middleton's introduction. "Guardian? What bloody guardian? If you're Security Service, why not just say so! I cannot remember a thing and I'm bloody sick of you people. Whatever happened, I cannot remember! Now, I'm on sick leave so please just bugger off!" He turned and went inside leaving a speechless Middleton on the doorstep. Gathering himself, Middleton turned and walked down the path before noticing the watching Sonya.

"Do you have the faintest idea what is going on here?" Sonya mutely shook her head. "Why doesn't that surprise me?" Middleton remarked and walked off, not knowing he had missed the chance to gain the whole story. Sonya watched him go with a slight frown and then looked back at the Police House. She saw Findlay gazing miserably out of a window and, suddenly resolute, marched up the garden path. Findlay took his time in answering her knock and regarded her with a faint scowl. "I could not help hear that man," Sonya announced.

"Only person you probably heard was me," Findlay retorted. "How can I help you, provided you are not a senior Police Officer, a member of the Security Services or a Journalist, that is!" Sonya gave him the benefit of one of her better smiles.

"I'm not, just someone who's a bit down and I couldn't help noticing you seemed even unhappier than me!" Findlay squinted at her.

"You are sane?" he enquired.

"Pretty well," Sonya informed him.

"Well, come and have a coffee, provided you don't ask questions!"

"Of course not," Sonya agreed and followed him into the house. He was, she had to admit to herself, extremely sexy.

While Sonya and Findlay became acquainted over a coffee, Detchant Middleton began to realise that there was a reason other than the threat of gagging orders that had led his fellow reporters to give up chasing the possibility of a story. Every attempt that he made to strike up a conversation was either ignored or brusquely terminated and he was sure that the shopkeeper had a gun held under the counter. When even a pleasant faced, well-dressed older woman with a terrier on a lead had responded to his

"Good Morning" by telling him to fuck off, he realised that he was going to struggle to find anything of value. It was with something approaching relief that he observed Fang approaching him. Despite the man's arrogance and assumption of superiority, at least he had spoken to him and, judging by the attitude of the locals, he could understand his surly nature. Trying to deal with that every day would make anyone rude.

"Ah, Middleton!" Fang was still playing his role of landed gentry as he felt it kept the journalist confused and too focused on the class war to see that he was bluffing. "Apologies for earlier, bad morning. Anyway, come for dinner tonight, about eight all right? Good." Fang walked off leaving Middleton speechless.

Well, if he wanted to play the squire, Middleton did not care. He would happily abuse his hospitality and worm the story out of him. He returned to his car to reread his notes and see if he could dredge up some details that would allow him to gain the upper hand with Fang. Despite himself, he found that he looked up from his note frequently to see if anyone was approaching his car. In the end, he drove off to try and find a quite spot to park up and consider what he had not found.

Back at Bleakhope, Alice sat outside the back door plotting the meal that she planned to give the journalist. Despite herself, she could not help smiling broadly at the thought of the future. All she had to do now was ensure that whatever story the journalist wrote up, they would be seen as innocent victims. The first step was to make the man feel off balance and what she planned to serve should help that.

Fang found himself whistling as he walked back up the drive. He decided that he had made the right decision in asking Alice to marry him and strangely neither the Police, the trainees or even the press seemed to be very important anymore. Not even the sight of a Coretec patrol as it cantered across the drive in front of him and back into the trees spoiled his mood. Arriving back at the house, he bent and kissed the sitting Alice for a long time before straightening and announcing he would help prepare the dinner for that evening. "No, there's no need, but you can keep me company while I get organised," Alice pulled on her rubber kitchen gloves and strolled off. Fang followed mystified. He knew Alice was a good cook but normally she turned the exercise into a mini drama.

Sitting in the Police House, Sonya was delighted to see that she could still interest a man. Findlay had definitely perked up over several coffees and some inane chatter. She suddenly had a flash of inspiration. "You really do look fed up!" she informed the smiling constable. "What on earth is wrong?" Despite himself, Findlay explained he had been concussed but, although he had been told that it was tackling a bunch of terrorists who were living undercover at the pub, he had no memory of the incident. "Poor thing," Sonya informed him and snuggled up against him, Findlay pretended not to notice and carried on with his explanation.

"It seems that there was a lot going on that the Security Services and the Antiterrorist Squad from headquarters missed, but they want to make sure I carry the blame. How the hell is a local policeman meant to spot a terrorist cell in deep cover when the specialists can't?" He paused as Sonya squirmed into his lap.

"You're very brave," she assured him and Findlay's ego joined his libido in putting in a reappearance. "But you'll have put them straight haven't you?" she enquired. Findlay deflated.

"Can't! I have lost my memory! I know I was worried about poachers and cattle thefts but that's all. They keep coming and suggesting that I made this mistake or that, but I know I didn't. Bloody frustrating though." Sonya took the time to kiss him.

"Well," she announced after several minutes, "we'll just have to put things together and make sure that the truth comes out. I'll help!" Findlay eyed her dubiously.

"Well, that might be a bit difficult, I mean I'm a police officer and…" Sonya silenced him with another kiss.

"Is there no one who acknowledges what you did or is on your side? Your sergeant or something?"

"Not a soul, other than the Inspector from CID and he can't buck the top brass or he'll lose his pension."

"There's your answer!" Sonya informed the bemused Findlay. "Give him a call and ask him to come over. I bet he tells you things off the record and we can pull together a dossier we can take to the press showing they cocked up totally and you did really well despite being left dangerously in the dark!"

"I don't know how you're going to manage that?" Findlay replied.

"Never mind, why don't you come for a meal tonight? You must be bored sitting on your own!" Despite himself Findlay agreed and she gave him directions. As she walked back towards Bleakhope, Sonya reviewed her plans with a smile. She was well aware that the original idea to have a training course had been hers and if she entangled the Police sufficiently, with luck they would never come close to identifying that fact. Secondly, she rather fancied him and it was a long time since a man had paid her much attention and third, it would give Fang, Alice and herself a good insight into what the Police thought.

The scene at Bleakhope moved rapidly from celebration to remonstration when the three realised what had been arranged without the others knowing. "You've invited that journalist?"

"Yes, but we didn't know you had asked the Police to dinner!"

"What the hell are we going to do?" Alice suddenly smiled.

"Well, it should convince both the Police and Middleton that we have nothing to hide at least. Anyway, let's have some champagne to celebrate our engagement! Then I'll cook."

"Ok, but I'll lay the table in the dining room."

"No way, we're eating in the kitchen tonight. Ian, is that home-made wine of your uncle's still there?" Fang sighed.

"You can't want to drink that! It's bloody potent and tastes like vinegar!"

"Brilliant! Just what I need." Fang sighed and looked at Sonya and shook his head.

"I give up. Tell me what you want and I'll do it but how this is going to sort out the press I don't know!"

"Trust me," Alice replied. As Alice busied herself at the stove, Fang set the table and Sonya wandered off humming to bathe and change.

Findlay was the first to arrive, rather shyly tapping at the door. He soon relaxed when he realised that Fang and Alice were approximately his age and happy to laugh at memories of university. He viewed the wine glasses and shook his head. "I'm not allowed to drink alcohol yet due to my concussion. Sorry." Fang smiled.

"Seeing what we will be drinking, I'd say it was a lucky escape! We're reduced to my late uncle's home-made wine and it's a bit wicked." Fang wandered over to Alice. "You still haven't told me how you're going to sort that bloody journalist and what's on the menu looks hellish!"

"I'm glad you think so or I'd be worried. Just wait and you'll see. I'll get Mr Guardian on our side." Just then, Middleton arrived and was quickly relieved of the bottle of decent red that he had brought. Middleton realised that he was somewhat over-dressed for the occasion as the others were wearing jeans and tee shirts while he was clad in chinos and a sports jacket. Strangely, Fang had lost his attitude and accent and Middleton was further discomforted to find that the quiet young bloke who smiled a lot was a policeman. His sense of disorientation increased when he realised that they were to eat in the kitchen. "Place is falling down and we are desperate to keep it going somehow," the by now well briefed Fang remarked. "We could have eaten in the dining room but the wood worm." He stopped speaking apparently embarrassed at mentioning such a problem. The soup was an interesting green and tasted distinctly alternative.

"It's nettle and dandelion," Alice informed them happily.

"How clever!" Sonya gushed.

"How the hell," Fang muttered unheard.

"Do you cook a lot of, ah, ecological food?" Middleton enquired.

"Too much!" Fang responded and watched Middleton choke on a sip of Chateau Bleakhope.

Findlay disgraced himself by breaking into hysterical giggles during the main course. Fang was vaguely appalled by the sight of the dish when it arrived, as it seemed to contain a variety of unidentifiable meats. "What is it exactly, darling?" he asked Alice. In response, she appeared to burst into tears and hid her face in her hands.

"I've tried, no money, nothing in the larder and guests for dinner!" Fang rolled his eyes.

"It's not that bad, after all, if the wretched clients for the training course would only pay their bills." Sonya interrupted him.

"They never will, they ignore us completely, disregard our instruction and direction, they just think they can do what they like!" Middleton watched and listened with interest.

"Oh, never mind all that!" Fang announced. "Have some casserole and drink up." He served everyone and Alice took her head out of her hands and smiled tearfully.

"Are you enjoying it?" she asked. Middleton wrestled manfully with a particularly horrible piece of gristle. He was beginning to feel sorry for her.

"Very pleasant. What do you call it?" Alice gave a shy smile.

"Oh, it's just something I threw together!" She gazed rather proudly at the pot. "I call it road kill." Both Fang and Middleton downed their glasses without hesitation and Sonya went vaguely pale. Alice glared at the giggling Findlay and looked back at Middleton. "Would you like some more?" she enquired. Middleton shook his head mutely and gratefully accepted another glass of wine and downed it hurriedly.

The sweet was also interesting and they looked at it with fascination. "And what do you, ah, call this, Alice?" Middleton enquired. By now the effect of the wine and her obviously brave attempt to cope despite their genteel impoverishment had softened his attitude.

"Oh, please, no more!" Findlay had shown a side of his nature that neither his colleagues, or the public, had ever seen. He viewed the whole evening as extremely entertaining and he had overheard far more of Alice's whispered instructions than he had been meant to. All in all, he was enjoying himself hugely and eager to see what happened next.

"Sorry! It must be my head injury. Sorry!" He subsided into helpless giggles once more until Sonya artlessly placed her hand in his lap and smiled sweetly.

"Well," Alice informed Middleton, "it's Apple Pie really."

"Is it? Oh, right!" They all looked at the strangely grey looking pastry.

"Well, the flour is home made and…"

"Home-made?" Fang interrupted. "Are you sure? If it's from the wheat in the old stable, we'll probably suffer from Ergotism!"

"I'm sorry, what's that?" Middleton was too interested to care about seeming less than all knowing.

"St Anthony's Fire. It's a fungus that grows on old grain and drives people mad. Quite prevalent in medieval France!" Middleton downed another glass of wine, no longer noticing the taste.

"Bring it on!" he announced and earned a happy smile from Alice.

"Ill get coffee," Fang announced rising from the table. "You don't mind ersatz do you? Made it myself from acorns from the wood."

Chapter 20

A grey day broke and seared brutally into the consciousness of the diners who had enjoyed the Chateaux Bleakhope. Only Findlay, at last finding a benefit from his head injury, was relatively unscathed. From various parts of the house, groans and retching signalled the start of the new day. The spaniel wandered from room to room, viewing the suffering dispassionately. It succeeded in rousing Fang with a particularly stomach churning stench based on finishing the remains of the casserole that it had found abandoned in the kitchen. "Oh God!" Fang moaned as he staggered downstairs to let the dog out. A happily exhausted Findlay appeared from Sonya's room looking for coffee.

"Do you have any of the real stuff?" he enquired. Fang nodded carefully.

"Yes, but make sure our friend from Fleet Street doesn't find out!" Findlay smiled.

"We need to have a word or two later," he informed Fang.

"Oh God. Later, ok, but not now, I think I am dying!" By the time Detchant Middleton managed to stagger into the kitchen, he found the others slowly recuperating and looking, despite their bedraggled state, better than he felt. Alice gave him a cup of Acorn coffee and guided him to a chair.

"Well, Detchant, you'd better ask your questions and we will give you a full explanation of how things have gone wrong. Constable Findlay can get an idea of what has been happening as well!"

While a slightly twisted version of events was being given at Bleakhope, grim reality continued to thunder across the landscape as Coretec and Fireflow devoted themselves to achieving supremacy. By now, the trainees bore no resemblance to their former selves and had adopted a vastly different approach to life than they had previously. Due to adapting their clothes to better suit their requirements, they were rapidly looking more and more like the original reivers. The men on both sides had padded their jackets with any material they could to help deflect blows from staves wielded by their opponents and a strange assortment of head protection had come to be worn. The women now wore a strange assortment of tattered dresses and skirts that exposed more than they hid. Almost to a woman they had found something that they wore as a shawl. In addition to losing whatever inhibitions they had originally had regarding blackmail and theft, the trainees' social mores had reverted to those of a harder time, quick to take offence and eager to avenge any slight. To anyone looking at them, they represented a frightening glimpse of the past that the watcher would have preferred not to see.

The Forty-Third Glasgow Scout troop was preparing to return to the city with mixed feelings. They all agreed that the camp had been educational but the fact that they had not achieved what they felt was worthwhile revenge on Coretec rankled. The Reverend McLeod had gone to say farewell to his colleague in the village and the students were in charge. "Aye, weel, we need tae sort those swine, but!" The lads agreed they needed sorting. After various ideas were proposed as to how to do Coretec. One of the students mentioned his disappointment with Fireflow as allies in their feud with Coretec. This in turn led to various ideas to teach Fireflow to be better allies in the future.

"Last time ah visited, yon big yin couldnae be bothered tae gie me the time of day!" Jamesie remarked.

"Right, this is what we'll dae!" The students seized command. The scouts listened intently and carefully memorised their instructions. "Mind, we dae this and awa' hame undetected! So, dinnae dae anything stupit!" They all nodded in agreement and went to prepare the trap for their enemies. In the best traditions of the Scouting movement, they planned to be prepared.

Coretec were aware that they were coming off worst in the escalating feud. Each clash seemed to result in their being forced to relinquish position or a client. The previous night had seen a successful lift of cattle from well outside their normal area of operations being forcibly taken from them by an overwhelming number of Fireflow riders. All those who had been present were nursing bruises and more than one glowered silently at Galphay. His position was weakening by the day and he now chose to sit apart from his heads of department who talked quietly amongst themselves with frequent glances towards his brooding figure. Finally, a deputation moved to stand around Galphay. He squinted at the bearded figures.

"What do you buggers want now?"

"Look, you need to do something to gain the upper hand. It can't go on like this. Last night showed yet again they're better led, better organised and we just get walked over. Sort it!" Galphay stood up menacingly but this had no effect on the new, harder, management team.

"Never mind the rant, just come up with an idea to win or we'll quit and join them. We lost another two last night and I bet they're celebrating they were captured!"

Furious at this blatant revolt, Galphay stormed out of the camp and raged through the woods. He stopped when he heard voices ahead and crept forward. Apparently unsuspecting, three scouts were crouched behind a bush gazing intently at the Coretec encampment. Without hesitating, Galphay grabbed the nearest and the other two sprinted off in apparent fright to report that the first part of the plan had been successfully implemented. It all depended on the acting skills of Jamesie now. Half an hour later, Snot trotted into the Fireflow encampment, and demanded to be taken to Mickley. A runner took the news that he was 'briefing' Mickley back to the students.

Back at Bleakhope, Detchant Middleton scribbled a last note and looked carefully at Alice. "And that's the whole story?" She nodded. "It seems so insane it has a horrible ring of truth and it's corroborated by two others so I'll accept it's the truth!" Alice wondered who the hell the corroborating witnesses were. Still, if for some unknown reason they backed up her tale she couldn't really care less. "Why have the Police not taken action? It just doesn't make sense." Middleton wondered.

"Well," Alice explained. "From what we can gather, not that anyone is talking, Constable Findlay..." She paused to check he was not in earshot, "got knocked out trying to break up a fight in the Sluggish Trout between the locals, Coretec and Fireflow. None of the locals want to say anything in case they are arrested for being involved. Also, the Security Services and the senior Police, seem to have overlooked a terrorist gang based at the pub and have concentrated all their efforts trying to get to the bottom of that, but seeing they killed all the terrorists ..." Middleton gaped at her.

"Killed all the terrorists? Without a trial and have kept it hidden?"

"It seems so." Alice agreed carefully.

"And I suppose they are trying to shift all the blame onto poor Findlay who was injured trying to protect his community! That's the real story, sorry Alice, you won't be getting many column inches!"

"You mean you're not going to write about us?"

"Look," Middleton explained. "There is a story about how a young couple just out of university and trying to preserve an ancient estate set up a training course that went wrong, but that's Sunday Supplement stuff and I don't do that. I'll certainly write how Coretec and Fireflow have gone mad and are playing at latter day reivers, but the main story will be about Human Rights, the Authorities operating a shoot to kill policy and their efforts to hide it by putting the blame on a courageous young officer who tried to uphold the law. As soon as I won't fail a breathalyser, I'll drive to the Police Headquarters and start asking questions. In the meantime I'll interview Findlay!"

The result of the apparent capture of a by now bitterly weeping Jamesie was to provide Coretec with a wealth of information concerning their rivals. Client farms, riding routes, their careful use of screening scouts to identify danger, were all exposed. Most importantly, Jamesie 'revealed' that Fireflow were planning to carry out a mass raid on Coretec that night with the intention of lifting all their cattle. A further shake convinced Jamesie to reveal that the scouts had advised them as to the best route to take to avoid detection on their ride and he was relatively easily persuaded to explain exactly what that was.

"Right!" Galphay informed his watching adherents. "Tie this little bastard up until we've sorted out his friends and get organised. We're going to take the buggers tonight and then there will be no more mention of getting things bloody sorted!" Jamesie was hauled off and they got down to organising the ambush.

Mickley listened carefully to Snot and tugged reflectively at his beard. "So, they are planning a full scale assault on our camp to lift the entire herd tonight?" Snot nodded. "And you managed to overhear them discussing their planned route of march?"

"Absolutely!" Snot agreed.

"Fascinating old boy. And, sadly your camp finishes today?" Snot agreed that this was indeed the case. "You'll be a loss to the community. Which scout troop are you exactly? I shall ensure we make a sizeable contribution to your funds when we have the chance." Snot departed smiling and waving to the friendly faces that saw him off. "Well, interesting snippet of news," Mickley announced. "We're going to be busy tonight! Now, listen, this is how we'll play it."

Amongst the noise and bustle of taking down the tents and carrying out a variety of checks for litter, lost equipment and unnecessary damage, the Reverend McLeod failed to realise that not every boy was in camp. The students considered how best to release Jamesie without alerting Coretec that it was a trap. They racked their brains without success when suddenly Jamesie appeared. "Bastards!" he announced.

"What happened?" Jamesie explained that he had been forced to divulge information as planned and had then been tied up.

"How come you're here then?" Jamesie smiled.

"Aye, well, ah said ah was awfae thirsty and that I couldnae feel my hands so one untied me so I booted him in rah crutch and ran!"

"Nice one!" They turned their attention once more to aiding their minister and soon there was nothing but lighter patches of grass to show that the scouts had ever been in the area.

Middleton finally drove off following a long conversation with Findlay that had mainly involved the constable refusing to answer any questions regarding the events in the area. He steadfastly stuck to the line that he could not discuss matters that were presently under investigation and referred Middleton to the Force headquarters. Finally giving up, Middleton drove off in search of answers and Findlay found himself back in Sonya's bed. A relieved Fang, having danced Alice around the kitchen in celebration, took her to the tower to talk without the risk of being overheard by Findlay. "He heard what you told me to do last night!" he explained. "He must have ears like a bat. Anyway, he

166

seems infatuated by Sonya and he told me that he wasn't going to help his superiors with anything he had discovered! He seems really quite bitter!"

"So what does he plan on doing?"

"Well, apart from trying to get Sonya to move in with him, he said as he can't remember anything he'll just have to start his investigations when he gets off sick leave. He seemed to pick up everything you told Middleton and thinks it's hilarious!" Fang shrugged. "I've no idea why, but he doesn't seem to care that we brought Bloody Coretec and Fireflow into the area but he does want revenge on them and the farmers for filling him in! Weird." Alice gave him a hug.

"And when are we going to get married?" Fang smiled weakly.

"Soon," he promised.

Coretec still tended to charge at everything without any thought of consequences, and their attempt to ambush Fireflow was no different. Ignoring the customary attempt by the Resources manager to try and provide some suggestion of how to improve their efforts, they cantered noisily into the dusk in a disorderly bunch. Back at the encampment, the Resources manager tried to organise his still jumbled thoughts without success. Angrily, he poked at the fire and wished that he could remember what was nagging at him but gave up. It was too late now in any event, they had all rushed off convinced that they knew what they were doing. He shook his head and went to check the cattle all memory of military tactics lost once more. Accordingly, it came as a total surprise to Coretec to find themselves suddenly assaulted as they moved into position to lie in wait for Fireflow. As it was, they were forced to string out where their route moved up a small but steep sided valley. At the worst moment for Coretec when they were virtually in single file, Fireflow rode down from either side, materialising out of the dark with disconcerting suddenness. Even Coretec's fearsome Operations team found themselves struggling just to stay in the saddle never mind take the fight to the opposition. In the end, Coretec avoided total defeat purely because the fight naturally moved down the slope onto more open ground where they were able to start supporting one another. Eventually, the mass of Coretec managed to break away and, rode for it.

Fireflow did not press home their advantage choosing instead to gather round their latest prisoners.

While Fireflow were enjoying their victory, Galphay tried to rally his team without success. "Look, you soft lot, if we ride like hell now, we can lift their entire herd! They'll be too busy telling each other how bloody clever they are!"

"Don't be daft!" Operations responded. "I give it five minutes for them to head for our base and lift all our cattle. We need to get back fast!" A chorus of agreement forced Galphay to back down and they retreated back to their encampment. The anticipated attack never happened as Fireflow had realised their own vulnerability and expected Galphay would do exactly what he had suggested. Also, despite their victory, most of them were nursing bruises as a result and did not fancy having them added to. In the end, other than a minor diversion to sweep up a small herd of cattle that they had spotted on their ride in, Fireflow returned straight to their base. The Scouts would have been delighted if they had seen how well their strategy had worked as represented by the bruised and battered state of both Coretec and Fireflow.

While Fireflow and Coretec were licking their respective wounds and considering their next move, Middleton was finding just how obdurate the Police and Security Services could be when they wanted to deny a story. After keeping him waiting for two hours they then informed him that they were unable to find the time to see him that day. In the meantime they had contacted his editor and carefully explained that they were taking the banning order very seriously and enquired if the editor really wished to experience prison life or to find himself suffering from a restraining order with regard to his movements and acquaintances.

"I'm sure home would become rather tedious after three or four years of not being allowed out, old boy!" The editor agreed and contacted Middleton hurriedly.

"Sorry Detchant, you can't investigate the security story any further!" He allowed Middleton to rant for a few minutes then explained the situation. "Look, neither of us wants to enjoy a forced sabbatical courtesy of a court order issued in a closed hearing! They are quite prepared to use antiterrorist legislation on us!" Middleton swore horribly. "I quite agree, but no more poking about up there! Now, was there a story or not regarding those IT companies?" Middleton explained the situation. "You mean, they've somehow got tangled up in the security scare? You can't publish anything then!" After further ravings from Middleton, the editor ordered him back to London. "We can review things properly when you get back and work out a plan to take things forward." Middleton was forced to agree.

Chapter 21

They formed little despairing groups who hid out in the woods and isolated stands of trees dotted around the Bleakhope estate. None could comprehend what had happened although they were all aware of the magnitude of the disaster. Fireflow, unusually, had been late in rising that morning. The knowledge that they had inflicted yet another defeat on Coretec and the consequential celebrations, had somehow lessened their usual drive. Also, for once Planning had made a mistake regarding the sentry rota and those who had ridden picket all night on the camp and herd, had not unnaturally come looking for their relief. A heated discussion had ensued and the new sentries were just saddling up when Coretec thundered into view.

Coretec, personified by the Operations team, were nothing if not resolute. Morning had found them moving stiffly around the camp and, seemingly innocently, discussing the situation with various small groups of colleagues. Invariably a member of Operations had instigated the conversation, let their colleagues vent their spleen on Galphay's leadership and then steered the conversation onto what total bastards Fireflow were. Only when the various participants anger had been fuelled by reminding them of the various humiliations and defeats that they had suffered at the hands of Fireflow, was any attempt made to suggest that a last, great effort be made to bring down the hated enemy. "If you think about it, the smug bastards will be sleeping late today after last night and we can get in amongst them before they know what's happening!" was the unvarying message. Despite all the evidence to the contrary, this idea met with approval from their colleagues. Finally, the Head of Operations drifted over to Galphay.

"Right, they're primed but you'd better win this time!" Galphay spat eloquently which the Head of Operations had found strangely cheering. It seemed the old sod had not lost his aggression anyway.

"Right, you buggers!" he bellowed. To a man and woman they roared their acclamation. If Coretec were going down to bloody ruin, it would be en masse. "Three pints of ale each and then we'll go and settle those bastards over the way!" Amidst further cheering, Galphay served them all ale himself. "Now drink up and let's get on with it!" Ten minutes later they had mounted up and, shouting their defiance, rode out to make their last throw of the dice. Even the Resources manager was mounted and swearing vengeance although on whom he could not remember.

Although the majority of Fireflow reacted quickly and ran to their ponies and indeed succeeded in mounting up in the face of the oncoming charge, they were in a disorganised mass rather than their normally carefully planned formation when Coretec hit. The effect was catastrophic, as the Fireflow riders were either knocked out the saddle with the initial impact or found themselves trying to fight two or three of Coretec's staff, single handed. The situation was made worse by Coretec's new tactic. The Resources manager had persuaded his colleagues to stop en route, and cut longish branches, explaining that this meant that they would be able to hit any opposition who were dismounted and to outrange their enemy when they were still in the saddle. The success of this approach was clearly seen as the fight raged out of the pony stockade and into the field containing the cattle, as screams, shouts and yells from victors and vanquished echoed off the distant woods. Soon, the fight resembled the conclusion of the Maxwell Johnston feud of the sixteenth century as Coretec rode past dismounted Fireflow riders and swung back handed at them with their sticks in a classical cavalry fashion. Skirmishing groups fanned out in all directions as Fireflow members fought frantically to escape and Coretec set about gaining their revenge.

It was exhaustion and drink that brought the fight to an end, that and the fact that those members of Fireflow who could, made their escape on horseback or on foot, generally into the woods where their pursuers chose not to follow. The remainder were either herded back to the camp if they could walk or left groaning and whimpering where they had fallen. Eventually, the Resources manager convinced Galphay that this was not acceptable, and prisoners were marshalled to retrieve their colleagues and provide first aid. Soon, Galphay enjoyed the pleasure of regarding the ranks of his defeated enemy who glared at him sullenly or sat mutely nursing their bruises. Not even the sight of several former Coretec employees amongst them spoiled his mood. "Daft buggers!" he remarked and then ignored them. "Where's their great leader then? I know he didn't escape because I belted the sod myself!" Operations dragged a reluctant Mickley forward.

"This one? I found him crawling around out there! What do you want to do with him?" For a moment the atmosphere seemed to chill as Galphay gazed malevolently at Mickley.

"Any suggestions?" he enquired menacingly. Mickley yawned and looked around and then back at Galphay.

"I'm sorry, did you say something?" Galphay laughed and clapped mockingly.

"Give the poor buggers something to eat and drink and kick them out. Not him though!" He pointed at Mickley. "He stays." He paused momentarily. "And his senior managers. Keep them under guard until later."

Considering the level of violence that had taken place, none of the combatants had suffered serious injuries and all were able to walk or be helped by colleagues out of the camp. Without leadership and dazed and dispirited, they too wandered into the woods to try and work out what to do next. In the main, this seemed to involve finding other colleagues to sit with and disconsolately compare cuts and bruises. Although their primitive armour had performed well, it had certainly not totally prevented injuries. The most disorientating thing for the broken ranks of Fireflow was the suddenness of their fall. One minute they had been riding high, with Coretec virtually finished, and control over the majority of the farmers in the area. Now, they had no food, few ponies and, they gradually realised, no friends. Certainly none expected anything but reprisals from the farming community and the village when the local population realised that their tormentors had been reduced to skulking in the woods. Interestingly, not one thought of heading to Bleakhope to try and resume their every day lives. The training had become their reality and so they skulked in the woods and looked for leadership.

Galphay seemed to have visibly grown with the victory. Having enjoyed a late breakfast on the meal cooked for Mickley, he swaggered over to the resentful figures of Fireflow's top management. "Happen they're not so bloody cocky now!" he remarked. His prisoners, to a man and woman, turned their backs on his grin. "Twats." He observed and wandered away. He was joined by his PA as he looked at the vast herd of cattle that Fireflow had gathered over the course of their activities. "Right, it's going to be a busy day! I want the two herds put together, that shower can stay with us for a while, might teach them to be less arrogant, and this place torched. Leave the ones that scuttled off nothing! Clear?" His PA nodded. "Right, and I want that done fast! Ask Operations and his lot to come and see me." He watched her head off and started to hum a strange little tune. The Operations team appeared and waited for him to pretend to notice them but for once were surprised when he immediately grinned at them. "Well done lads, good work that!" They smiled back, delighted at this sudden praise. "Now, I've been thinking and I want to ram home to that bloody Fang we've won big time. Understand?"

Within the hour, Coretec were on the move once more, resembling something out of the historical mists, they rode around the cattle while their prisoners stumbled behind their ponies pulled by ropes tied around their wrists. Far ahead, the Operations team were galloping towards Bleakhope tower itself while others were riding furiously back to their base to fetch their herd. Fang gazed down from the battlements of the tower at the unfolding scene in total disbelief. "What the fuck..." he muttered before turning and rushing down the stairs and into the open. Before he could go in search of Alice, he was surrounded by Coretec's Operations team who merely smiled nastily when he demanded what they were playing at. Galphay's arrival did not at first make matters any clearer. His response to Fang's furious enquiries took the form of a cryptic "Wrapping it up." Fang swore furiously and tried again.

"What the hell are you planning on doing with all those cattle and..." Words failed him when the bound and dishevelled figures of Fireflow's senior management were dragged into view. Fang gazed at them in horror and turned to Galphay. "You can't string them up!"

"I know, pity!" Galphay regarded Fang carefully. "What we are doing is ensuring there is no dubiety regarding who has won." Fang looked at the prisoners and then back at Galphay.

"No, I'd agree with that statement." Galphay shook his head.

"Not yet! There's another five days to go! By the time we finish, there won't be any debate. Now, I want your tower so I'm taking it!" He held up a hand to still Fang's furious protests. "Look, I'm asking politely or you can join them if you'd rather. Anyway, I need somewhere to keep them and we need more grazing for the beasts. Around here will be just fine!" When an incoherent Fang raged off to find Alice, Galphay issued further orders to Operations.

The local farming community were not amused when Coretec appeared that day demanding further protection fees in the form of livestock from every farmer that had been under Fireflow's suzerainty. "Shouldn't have trusted those losers!" Was the closest they got to a sympathetic response. While Coretec busied themselves in taking over the Fireflow operation as proof of their victory, some of their colleagues were creating a new camp around Bleakhope tower and blocking off its long open entrances with timber they dragged from the yard. Fang watched impotently from the house with Alice as they did so.

"What the hell can we do?" Alice enquired. Fang shrugged.

"Suffer I suppose." He paused momentarily and gave her a hug. "Don't worry too much, that idiot always oversteps the mark and cocks up! When are Findlay and Sonya due back?" Alice shook her head.

"I really don't know. They said they were off to sort out a dossier. Sonya said she had an idea that would fix his problems with his bosses." Fang burst out laughing despite himself.

"Poor bastard! It was her idea to bring this lot here!" Alice half giggled.

"Well, he'll have an exciting career while it lasts!" Eventually they decided to go to the Police House to see what the others thought of the latest development. Fang took the time to explain to Galphay that while the use of the tower could somehow be seen as acceptable, anyone entering the house would be treated as a criminal.

"And I don't mean by the law," he assured him meaningfully.

When Fang and Alice walked down the drive, they were unaware that several former Fireflow riders watched them from the trees where they had spent most of the day lurking and considering their options. Now that the Fireflow leadership was gone, the tendency had been to split into even smaller groups and to move away from each other. All the cohesion that had been their great strength was lost and each little made its own decisions, often inadvertently foiling the efforts of others. All over the estate, two or three 'broken men' had created hidden encampments. It had not taken long for them to realise the full extent of their defeat when they had tried to return to their former base and found it destroyed and all the livestock gone. The few that had managed to escape on their ponies not unnaturally saw any pedestrian colleagues as a threat and rode further away. As they realised that they were only going to eat by stealing food, while also being fully aware that they dare not go near farms or the village where they had little doubt that the population would turn on them, so the number of attempted thefts at isolated houses in the area rose dramatically.

While what remained of Fireflow were ensuring that they rapidly achieved a pariah like status, Fang and Alice explained the latest events to Findlay and Sonya.

"Anyway, with any luck they'll keep out the house," Fang remarked and thought for a moment. "In fact, I'm positive they will because I don't think they see themselves as being part of our lifestyle anymore."

"Eh?" Findlay failed to understand Fang's ramblings.

"Well, I don't think they see themselves as part of modern society anymore! I honestly think they have developed into reivers – we've trained them too well! So, modern things are of no interest including the house!" Findlay groaned.

"I hopefully get off sick leave in the next day or two and the place is stuffed with hooligans who see themselves as reivers. Thanks a lot!" They all looked at each other and Fang, Sonya and Alice fervently prayed that Findlay would somehow lose them from any explanation as to why he required reinforcements to tackle the triumphant Coretec. Almost in unison, they all sighed as they considered the latest situation. "Damn them, I'll just play sick for a bit longer!" Findlay announced. "Anything might happen to sort things without me having to get involved." The others merely looked worried.

Back at Bleakhope, several of the prisoners were also becoming concerned. It was becoming apparent that Galphay had no intention of releasing them to renew hostilities. The senior management team found themselves shut in a damp, dark room with a crude door fashioned from appropriated timber and guarded at all times by three of Coretec's staff armed with sticks. Mickley had been placed on the roof where he had no hope of escaping and Galphay enjoyed visiting him at frequent intervals to explain how easy it had been to defeat him and share any interesting developments such as another farm now paying blackmail that had been formerly on Fireflow's books or the easy defeat of a pathetic assault by two or three escapees. It made for a very long day for the defeated.

In the Police House, Fang and the girls had fallen silent when the Inspector had visited Findlay to see how he was doing.

"A lot better, sir. I was just telling my friends that I hoped to get back to work in the next day or two." The Inspector grunted.

"See how you feel in the morning, it was a nasty injury you took. Not that we don't need you, there seems to be a crime wave at the moment." The inspector paused and motioned Findlay to follow him out of earshot of the listeners. "I really would consider your return carefully," he informed Findlay. "The district is in uproar and the top brass are keen to blame anyone but themselves for what happened. While you are an officer injured in the course of duty it's difficult for them to really push you forward as a scapegoat, but a fit officer on duty?" He let his words hang. Findlay smiled wanly.

"I understand. But, sir, what if it was suggested that I had a dossier that proved my innocence and their culpability?" The inspector whistled.

"They'd be damned careful what they did, but I wouldn't give it up to them in a hurry."

"No, quite, but if you were to tell them that I had placed it with my solicitor for safe keeping? Not that I would ever disclose it to the press or anything" The inspector chuckled quietly.

"I don't think there would be quite the same keenness in laying the blame at your door. Do you have such a dossier?" Findlay smiled.

"Certainly, and it's with my lawyers who I also gave the name and contact details of my friend Detchant Middleton of the Guardian in case they should ever want to contact him." The inspector smiled nastily.

"Well, I look forward to seeing you back on duty in a couple of days. In the meantime I want to have a chat with that charming Chief Constable of ours."

That night, Findlay's solicitors were broken into and their premises rifled although the subsequent Police investigation turned up no clues as to the perpetrators. More strangely, the solicitors could not find anything missing although the Chief Constable endured a long conversation with London over a secure line. Even stranger, Findlay merely laughed when the inspector told him of the event and seemed remarkably unconcerned. Instead, he gave Sonya a hug and took to humming 'Smoke gets in your eyes' frequently.

Chapter 22

For two days, Coretec enjoyed their unchallenged position as principle 'riding family' in the worst of traditions. They swaggered through the village, paid constant bullying visits to farms to demand ever more tribute and enjoyed humiliating their prisoners. By now, it seemed the only thing that interested them was counting the numbers of cattle that they held in lowing confusion and ensuing the local population knew that they were in control. Even Archie despaired, and a number of his colleagues openly blamed him for their troubles. "If yon bugger hadn't twatted the polis we'd no be in this fix," became a frequently heard refrain. As it was, Findlay showed no seeming interest in returning to work, spending his time either at Bleakhope obviously buttering up to the gentry, or sleeping late with his new bidey in.

The Women's Guild's plans had failed miserably. The intention had been for Deirdre to exercise her undoubted charms in leading either Mickley or Galphay astray while Jeannie, using her skills as a wild life photographer to capture this and threaten to show the results to Deirdre's extremely large and viciously jealous husband. Unfortunately, it had proved impossible to get close to either of their intended victims and, worse, a form of trial run that had involved the unknown Management Trainee from Fireflow, had made the pair alter their intentions completely. Having both found the exercise somewhat stimulating and then discovered that the film, when inadvertently found, had certainly interested their respective husbands, they were proving a danger to their erstwhile colleagues in the Guild as they developed a stunning series of pornographic films starring other women's husbands to brighten up the winter evenings. When Jeanie's partner later came up with the bright idea of marketing the films, the quartet became seriously wealthy.

With the Police, Farmers, Women's Guild and other potential leaders of any fight back at best disinclined, at worst unable, to tangle with Coretec, their continuing rule of terror seemed likely to continue unchecked. As so often in history, it was the Church that answered the call of the people and organised resistance. The fact that this was in fact an inadvertent act did not detract from its results. The local minister had been very taken with the young Reverend McLeod. He had found his youthful enthusiasm and sound theological views a refreshing change to those of his more world-weary colleagues and had extended an invitation to come and preach at the Parish Church. McLeod, feeling deeply honoured, had accepted with alacrity. Further, he had wondered if he might speak on the day that the Kirk planned to launch its 'Direct Action by Church Goers for Peace' initiative. Smiling to himself at McLeod's boyish enthusiasm, he had happily assented. Unusually, the minister had exerted himself to interest his congregation in McLeod's visit. Further, he had used the broad nature of the sermon to invite his colleagues at the Roman Catholic Chapel and the Episcopal Church, to join the service. The result was that when McLeod stood up to preach, he gazed in wonder at rows of crowded pews, not realising that not all were adherents of the Church of Scotland, and was inspired.

"For too long!" McLeod thundered, "the Church in its broadest sense, has failed to stand up to tyranny. It has failed to be a good shepherd to its flock! We have failed to defend what we know is right, choosing rather to appease and avoid. Before the Good Samaritan appeared" He paused, startled by loud clapping from the congregation then pressed on with his message. Whistles and cheers issuing from the building startled a lone tourist passing the Church. McLeod spoke eloquently and movingly for thirty minutes regarding the Church's failings to stand up to oppression. The fact that he was speaking with the trouble spots of the world in mind was totally lost on his listeners who took his words to refer to their own situation. When McLeod finally wrapped up his sermon with the exhortation to "Take the fight to Satan wherever he may be and in whatever shape he may take"! The congregation stood and roared their agreement. After the service, and as the congregation rushed furiously away through the churchyard in excited groups, McLeod smiled at his colleagues. "I'm not used to such, ah, congregation participation, but I appreciated their willingness to listen to my poor efforts." His three professional colleagues gaped at their normally staid parishioners, several of whom seemed to be pulling up Church palings while others appeared to be marshalling the rest into a cohesive unit before they all moved off chanting. "What are they saying?" McLeod wondered. "I can't quite make it out." The Priest crossed himself.

"It sounded awfully like Death! Death! To me," the clerics regarded one another uneasily.

Findlay heard the sound of the approaching mob and stepped outside his house and gazed in amazement as what seemed like the entire population stormed up the road towards him, waving sticks, fence palings, umbrellas and bibles. "What the hell?" he wondered and, obviously not having learnt from his past experience, moved to stand in front of them. "And what are you planning?" he enquired. They stopped momentarily and he shuddered despite himself as they glared at him.

"We are marching in support of Direct Action by Church Goers for Peace!" he was informed.

"Ah, well, just keep it peaceful will you?" The mob nodded and he was relieved to spy several of the more sensible of the community in their ranks. Findlay watched them move off up the road and wondered where they planned on going. There was nothing in that direction but open countryside. Deciding that the predominantly middle-aged march would soon tire, he went back inside to Sonya.

Fang was wandering angrily around the yard in front of the house and casting furious glances at Bleakhope tower when he heard the faint hum that was the approaching Church Goers for Peace. Instantly assuming that this was some further lunacy being perpetrated by Coretec, he stormed off to investigate the noise. Alice glimpsed him passing the window and sighed. Just when she thought she had got everything sorted, Coretec had taken over the tower. She had not realised how much Fang cherished the place and, while the interlopers were in occupation, she knew there was no hope of her furthering her marriage ambitions. The spaniel whining to be let out brought her back to the present and, when she opened the back door for the dog to bustle out and away down the drive after Fang, she heard the approaching crowd who were now much louder and their chants of "Death! Death!" chillingly clear.

Fang's angry walk slowed as he caught site of the advancing Church Goers and finally stopped when he made out their shouts.

"What the hell is going on now?" he wondered. The spaniel joined him and he was strangely grateful for its support as it sat down next to him and licked itself loudly. The mob advanced on him, still chanting, and Fang noticed their assortment of weapons with growing alarm. Finally they stopped in front of him and shouted "Death!" three times before subsiding into a terrifying silence. Fang cleared his throat and the spaniel stopped licking.

"What, may I ask" Fang paused to swallow. "What are you doing?" The unmistakeable figure of the local solicitor pushed himself forward.

"We," he announced, "Are Direct Action by Church Goers for Peace!" Silence fell once more. Fang gulped audibly then summoned his courage.

"Then why are you on my land?" The rather portly solicitor seemed to swell with indignation.

"You brought Satan into our midst and we are going to take the fight to him!" Fang inadvertently took a step back.

"Satan? Here? I hardly think so." The marchers started chanting deafeningly and the spaniel looked up at Fang then back at the Church Goers. The solicitor held up a hand and silence fell once more.

"If you do not stand aside, it is obvious that you support Satan. We are going to beat Him out of the area and all who support him!" The spaniel farted eloquently and abandoned Fang to his theological debate. Fang, with an aplomb that would have impressed his ancestors, smiled wickedly and stepped to one side.

"I believe you will find him in the tower," he pointed helpfully. "Not the house," he called urgently as the mass moved forward. Suddenly fearful for Alice, he sprinted past the leaders and followed the spaniel back up the drive.

Coretec were participating in humiliating the senior management team of Fireflow who, Galphay had announced, were to be released that day with the exception of Mickley. Rather than merely release their prisoners, Coretec had assembled around the tower, and formed a menacing corridor of mounted riders that the unfortunate Fireflow managers had to pass through to reach freedom. Their erstwhile jailers enjoyed themselves shouting abuse and pretending to swing their clubs at them to make them jump around to avoid being hit. Galphay was standing at the entrance with the faithful Operations team enjoying the spectacle. Due to the noise that they were making, no member of Coretec heard the sound of the approaching Church Goers for Peace until it was too late.

Galphay gaped in amazement as the Church Goers suddenly erupted into view, their faces contorted with hate as they brandished their weapons and chanted their war cry of "Death! Death!" As the slowest Coretec staff member realised his colleagues had stopped shouting and tormenting the prisoners and fell silent, so the Church Goers also ceased to shout. Instead they halted and spread across the open space that led from the tower and into the surrounding countryside. Coretec looked at each other, at Galphay and then back to the silently menacing throng. The suddenly forgotten Fireflow prisoners gazed in horror, then, showing remarkable self-preservation, sprinted back towards the tower. Seeing them come, Galphay stepped back behind his Operations team who closed ranks to bar admittance. For a moment, the erstwhile prisoners pleaded to be let back into the tower then fell silent as the solicitor bellowed into the silence.

"There! There he is! Satan and all his minions! Smite in the name of the Lord!"

As the Church Goers for Peace broke into a charge, intent on taking Direct Action, Galphay and the Operations team stepped smartly through the door and slammed it shut. As the Coretec riders found themselves surrounded by a baying mob that instantly set about trying to drag them off their horses, the Fireflow management team clutched each other before Marketing screamed,

"Act like them! Come on, it's our only hope!" In desperation the others did as instructed and assaulted the nearest Coretec rider. The suddenness of the assault and the restricted area in front of the tower meant that Coretec found themselves without their normal advantages of speed and movement. Instead, each of them was surrounded by a furious know of Church Goers who flailed at them or else tried to drag them off their terrified ponies. Several riders were pulled screaming off their horses while their colleagues found themselves hemmed in and forced to stand in their stirrups and desperately rain blows with their sticks at their assailants. The solicitor and several others reeled back bleeding profusely from scalp wounds but this just seemed to encourage the others to intensify their assaults.

A Coretec accountant managed to force himself out of the mob by cutting down right and left then kicking his pony forwards. As soon as he had space to gain momentum, he reined round and thundered back into the melee. Within moments, several other Coretec riders, due to his intervention, had managed to free themselves and, forming a tight phalanx, they counterattacked. Momentarily, the battle hung in the balance but, just as Coretec seemed to be about to gain the upper hand due to the efforts of the accountant, the chairwoman of the Woman's Guild, shrieking incoherently, swung her umbrella mightily and knocked the accountant off his pony. Seeing their new champion bested, Coretec lost heart and cohesion. With their lost unity, they fought only to escape. A number succeeded in forcing their way through the Church Goers, but the majority were rapidly overwhelmed.

An appalled Galphay stared down at the utter defeat of his riders. With startling suddenness, the fight was over. A few riderless ponies cantered around then found their way out into the fields. Coretec employees either sprawled groaning on the ground or were fiercely gripped by still powerful middle-aged parishioners. The chairwoman of the Woman's Guild peered at the bloodied figure of the solicitor and assumed control.

"Hold them firm mind!" she shouted and, resembling something out of the Old Testament, turned to the tower. Galphay quailed under her gaze. "Oh Lord!" the chairwoman bellowed. "See fit to rid the country of Satan and his supporters!" She pointed at Galphay. "Curse you!" she screamed. "Curse you when you wake and when you sleep!" She went on in a similar vein for several minutes. Galphay was too horrified to do anything but watch and listen. If her words proved prophetic his last hours were fast approaching and likely to be extremely unpleasant. Eventually, the chairwoman ended her impassioned speech. The mob then bowed their heads in prayer before organising themselves.

Leaving thirty to guard the tower, the rest of the Church Goers, still holding their prisoners and ably assisted by the Fireflow managers, marched away singing Onward Christian Soldiers lustily. Fang, an arm round Alice's shoulders, watched them march past still singing.

"Like Cromwell's New Model Army!" he remarked. Alice looked at him. "No, you're right!" Fang stated although she had said nothing. "More militant than them." Findlay was sprawled happily on the settee with Sonya when he heard the sound of singing.

"The Church March must be coming back," he remarked. "I'd better take a look." He pulled on his trousers and wandered outside. To his amazement, the marchers had obviously been in a fight. Many were cut, almost all were dirtied and their clothes were torn. Even more surprising, they were dragging a number of badly beaten individuals with them, in several cases actually having to hold them upright.

"What in God's name have you been up to?" Findlay demanded.

"In God's name, the now recovered solicitor informed him, "we have been carrying out His wishes!" The captives were shoved towards him or dropped, dependent upon their condition. Findlay looked at these unfortunates then back at the crowd.

"There will be no mob rule here!" He announced and found himself totally ignored. "I said," he started again then, seeing that they were all looking past him, turned to see what they were staring at. Sonya was standing in the doorway gazing amazed at the scene. Findlay rose to the occasion. "My fiancée," he announced to Sonya's delighted amazement. "Sonya, put some clothes on and come and meet the village." She vanished with a squeak and the crowd turned their attention on Findlay once more. "Explain what you have done to these people!" he commanded.

Thirty minutes later, the small cell attached to the Police House was filled with Coretec employees. Findlay had declared himself fit for duty and was demanding that the prisoners be removed to more suitable accommodation, while Sonya, following his instructions, noted the names and addresses of the Church Goers so that they might be interviewed by Findlay for future statements. Once they had been processed, the Church Goers reformed and marched back to the Church and held an impromptu prayer meeting. The clerics wisely stayed away, choosing instead to discuss good and evil amongst themselves. The Reverend

McLeod had wanted to join the congregation but his wiser colleagues had counselled against it.

"It will only encourage them," remarked the Parish Priest. "It's easier if you think and they listen, you'll find."

Meanwhile, the Coretec escapees had rapidly met their erstwhile enemies from Fireflow while fleeing through the countryside. Strangely, the feud seemed to have been lost in their mutual defeat and without the twin catalysts of Mickley and Galphay. Recognising that they were all hunted now, they decided to work together. That night, a lightning raid on Bleakhope ensured that they all had ponies if little else.

Galphay watched the raid ride in and, at first, thought they had come to rescue him. Showing commendable steadiness, the besiegers had formed up in front of the tower, but none of the whooping riders had come close. Instead they had thundered by and rounded up as many ponies as they could before vanishing into the dark. Galphay had rounded cursing on the Operations team and Mickley. The Operations team had glowered and Mickley laughed delightedly. Shortly thereafter, food and reinforcements had arrived from the village. The night had passed in prayer and hymn singing to the Tower's inhabitants' fury.

Chapter 23

Findlay's sudden return to duty discomfited a number of people. It also brought an abrupt end to the reiver revival. The Inspector had thoroughly enjoyed the panic caused by the suggestion that Findlay had a dossier of evidence that clearly showed culpability in the senior ranks and the Security Services. Indeed, by the time he left the head quarters building, he was rather worried that he had overplayed his hand. The report of a spate of burglaries at solicitors' offices in the area told him he had not. Attitudes seemed to have changed rapidly and Findlay's return to duty was broadcast as exciting news rather than a spur for Standards to demand he visit them for interview. The headquarters cells were now packed with Coretec staff meaning that the normal offenders had to be relocated within the area, either in cells under the Sheriff's court or in larger sub stations. Adding to the burden on the uniform branch was the outcome of Findlay's rapid investigations.

Every member of the Direct Action by Church Goers for Peace had been interviewed and statements taken within three hours. Findlay had then used the information he had gained on the activities of both Coretec and Fireflow to visit a sampling of farms to establish the extent of the rustling, protectionism and arson that had occurred while he had been off duty. Making it plain that he understood the initial reticence regarding his injury and did not intend to take any further action seemed to permit the farmers to admit to a certain degree of problems. Once Findlay assured them that it was highly unlikely the Security Services would wish to dig any deeper into the terrorist incident as it would highlight their own failings rather than the criminal activities of the locals, and that the initial brawl could be seen as self-defence on the part of the NFU, the floodgates opened.

Findlay had furiously typed up a report, listing the witnesses, a sample of the offences and, after further discussion with Sonya, Alice and Fang, the identities of the Coretec and Fireflow gangs.

He also laid down the level of support that he would need to re-establish the rule of law. It was this list of demands that ensured the telephones rang late into the night across the country as various forces, near and far, were contacted for assistance and resulted in the overtime bill to the force escalating rapidly. Finally, Findlay received the call he had been awaiting ever since a fleeting visit to Bleakhope tower. When he replaced the telephone receiver he had beamed at Sonya who gazed admiringly back at him. "Dawn! That's when it all kicks off! There will be quite a lot of people coming and going tonight so you might be better sleeping back at the big house." Sonya made a face but agreed to do as he requested. "Make sure you are awake at first light though! I wouldn't want you to miss anything." He refused to tell her any more and drove her back to Fang and Alice before disappearing into the night. "One last job and then I will wait for others to take over!" he had informed Sonya.

Archie was not happy when he opened his door at midnight in response to the thunderous knocking on his door and the barking of his dogs. "Whit the..Oh, it's you officer." Findlay ignored the pleasantries and grabbed Archie by the throat and lifted him off the step.

"If you ever even look the wrong way at me in future I will make your life a living hell! I'll let you off with clobbering me because everyone swears it was an accident but push me, and you'll suffer a few 'accidents' on the way to the cells!" He gave Archie a shake to underline his words. Archie, unable to speak, managed to nod and Findlay dropped him. "Well, goodnight then." Findlay drove off as Archie picked himself up.

"Bastard!" he muttered and went inside massaging his throat. "Maybe I should try tae get him down the rugby club, though?" Archie wondered as he returned to his bed.

Sporadically through the night, heavy vehicles moved carefully through the village and stopped with a hiss of air brakes at the Police House. The Inspector had appeared to nominally take charge but left Findlay to it and merely sat drinking tea and offering advice and authority when it was needed. "Your doing fine. I'll just take a watching brief and any credit," the inspector informed Findlay. "Explain your planning again so I can answer any whining from on high." Findlay had grinned and done so. An hour before dawn the Inspector stirred himself. "Right, final briefing and we'll get moving," he announced. Findlay sighed; he had known it was too good to last. "Right, ladies and gentlemen, shut up and listen! Constable Findlay, it's his area, will brief you as to the operation. Any questions, keep them to the end. Findlay?" Findlay stood up and started to talk. His colleagues listened at first sceptically then with growing enthusiasm.

The village woke early to the clatter of hoofs as horses were led out of horse boxes and mounted all along the road to the Police House. Lights came on and curtains twitched as the residents looked out to see what was happening. The Mounted Inspector looked with pride at his command. Every Mounted Section in Scotland had been drafted in to help hunt down the remnants of Coretec and Fireflow. As they were released from their vans, the police dogs that were to be used as trackers snapped and snarled with excitement. Suddenly the noise was drowned out by a large military helicopter that clattered low over the village then swept up and into a hover over Bleakhope tower.

Findlay, standing with the sentries from the Church Goers outside Bleakhope tower, watched in admiration as the antiterrorist squad abseiled out of the helicopter and dropped onto the roof of the tower. A succession of loud explosions as the troops entered the building made him wince. Shouts and screams echoed from within and then, within moments, the watchers were deafened and dazzled by a further explosion as the door was blown off the entrance by another squad of soldiers who vanished inside. A minute later, Findlay happily took custody of Galphay, Mickley and the Coretec Operations team while the Church Goers applauded politely. Fang pounded round the corner, closely followed by Alice and Sonya. They watched as the prisoners, hands bound with plastic ties, were made to sit on the ground to await transport. "Morning," Findlay announced as the troops emerged and vanished through the trees to where they could re-board the helicopter.

It was the barking of the dogs that first alerted the broken elements of Coretec and Fireflow that something was happening. Most had been aware of the increased heavy traffic in the area, but had not perceived it as any threat. The sound of the police dogs had a very different effect. Senses and instincts had been fine tuned during the course of the past weeks and the trainees did not waste any time in discerning a possible threat. Almost to a man and woman, they started to wakefulness and mounted up. Due to the previous evening's raid on Bleakhope they all had a pony and had been planning a raid that day to try and restore some semblance of control. Instead, a frisson of fear ran through them all as they sensed they had become hunted.

"Ride!" An unknown voice yelled and they bomb burst from their laager and cantered off across country in all directions.

The dogs dragged their handlers into the wood while behind the mounted Police were forced to duck under branches and restrain their overexcited horses who sensed the dogs wish to hunt. They reached the recently vacated sleeping area and, almost immediately, snarls and screams announced that the dogs had caught a fugitive. The Resources manager, who still struggled with the results of his concussions, had failed to wake when his colleagues had fled. The first indication that he had of the Police activity was when several excited German Shepherds bit him. By the time the dogs were driven off, he was wide- awake and well mauled. He was carried out of the woods groaning with pain by two burly handlers whose dogs walked snarling at their heels.

"You shouldn't have resisted arrest." he was informed. "It makes the dogs overexcited." Faced with this flawless logic, the Resources manager did not bother to respond other than groan.

The rest of the Police contingent were by now forcing themselves out of the trees and into the open as they followed the dogs that were obviously on a hot scent. It quickly became apparent that their quarry had split up as the dogs started moving in different directions so the Inspector divided his force so that each trailing hound was followed by several mounted Police as well as its handler. The keenness of the dogs communicated itself to the mounted Police who urged their handler colleagues to speed up. They tried with varying success dependent on their age and fitness. So, with gathering pace, the hunt set off in pursuit to the increasing distress of the handlers.

Findlay, by now back at the Police House, drank coffee with the Inspector and listened to developments crackle over the radio.

"So far.." he murmured.

"Aye, well, now we just wait," the Inspector informed him. "The boys will be having a fine time! I'd better call himself and say it's all going to plan. You make sure our prisoners get bussed over to headquarters." Findlay was organising the shepherding of Mickley, Galphay and the Operations team into two vans, when the Resources manager was carried into view. They all stopped and gazed in horror at the sight.

"Resisted arrest!" a handler informed Findlay. "Had to use a dog to restrain him." The prisoners hurriedly climbed into the vans as the dogs grew closer.

"No problems?" a handler enquired.

"Not so you'd notice". Findlay replied.

By now, all but two of the dog handlers were suffering badly from the pace they were being forced to set. Their attempts to claim that the dogs were outrunning their noses were manifestly untrue and treated with derision by their horse borne colleagues. Each group solved the problem in different ways. Several handlers clutched the stirrup of a mounted colleague with either hand and, with the dog's leash tied to their waist, bounded across the county. This system worked well until the trail they followed crossed a fence or dry stone wall or entered a wood. One groaning handler suffered having his dog being released by overexcited colleagues who abandoned him lying amongst the remains of the wall he had tried to leap unsuccessfully. Other, lighter dog handlers were now on horseback, seated behind colleagues and clinging on desperately to dog leash and rider alike. In this fashion, the chase speeded up and the Police closed rapidly on their quarry as the larger police horses rapidly overtook the smaller ponies of the fugitives.

Soon, the first captures began to be made. A mounted contingent surrounded a small thicket that the dog led them to and called for anyone hiding to show themselves. The answer they received was a sudden charge by two Coretec riders who, recognising they were finished, chose to go down fighting. The Police drew their long batons in response to the sticks wielded by Coretec and it was all over on moments. Draping their prisoners over their ponies, the Police radioed in their success and a warning that the fugitives were likely to be violent.

Four others were captured on being flushed from hiding in some dead ground, the fourth only after a furious chase when she twisted and turned like a hare pursued by long dogs, dodging from under the noses of the Police horses at the last moment. Finally, her pony stumbled with exhaustion and they rode her down. Matters then became confused as the wildly overexcited Police dog flew indiscriminately at all concerned as soon as they dismounted to arrest her. Finally, a mounted officer used a can of Mace on the dog and was punched by its handler in retaliation.

While the majority of the 'broken men' were captured comparatively quickly, those who evaded capture indulged in an orgy of destruction where they could before they too were hunted down. Several hay barns went up in flames and sheep, cattle, including a bull and free range hens were all liberated. The police dogs present acted with admirable restraint in the face of the sheep and poultry but the appearance of an angry bovine intent on defending his herd seemed to trigger an atavistic memory. To an animal, they tried to close with the bull despite the best efforts of their handlers. This led the bull to charge in retaliation and the pursuit turned into a shambolic retreat. When they finally regrouped, both humans and animals were badly shaken.

"What the fucking hell were you thinking?" an angry handler demanded of his dog. He received no response; the dogs were still gazing longingly in the direction of the furious bovine obviously keen to try conclusions.

By nightfall, it was all over. The power of Coretec and Fireflow had been smashed and the twenty-first century had returned to Bleakhope. Findlay was sat at his PC starting to try and write a sensible record of all that had happened. The prisoners seemed almost dazed as if in shock. In the majority of cases, they seemed unable to grasp that they had broken the law or behaved in anything but a normal fashion. The press had returned with a vengeance and were scouring the area for stories and interviews. Fang and Alice were ensuring with Sonya that their stories continued to match and what to do next while waiting for Findlay to join them to celebrate his triumph and their engagement. The district was settling for its first undisturbed night since Coretec and Fireflow had commenced training.

Chapter 24

Six months later, and early spring was making its presence felt on the Bleakhope estate. There had been considerable changes following the fall of Fireflow and Coretec. Guided by Sonya, Fang had sold the tale of the training exercise that had gone wrong to the press. To his amazement this had brought in considerable amounts of money that meant he was able to renovate the house and spend money on the farm and outbuildings. To his and Alice's delight, they now had money in the bank. Even more exciting, following a number of transatlantic telephone calls, a producer was due in from the US to discuss buying the rights to the story in order to make a film. Alice observed that this was unlikely to bear any resemblance to the truth.

"Thank God!" Fang replied, still conscious that he might yet be dragged into the courts to answer awkward questions. Alice merely smiled, she was too happy with her newly married status.

The local farming community was not so contented. When they had submitted their myriad of claims for criminal damage, theft of livestock and arson attacks, the Insurance Companies had cited their exclusion clauses that referred to Civil Disturbance and terrorist activity. Despite the best efforts of the NFU and sundry lawyers, this decision remained unchanged and it did not seem likely that it ever would. It was difficult to deny that there had been terrorist activity and where that had ended and the activities of Fireflow and Coretec had begun was hard to say. For example, Archie had been nearly reduced to incoherent rage debating if the fire that had occurred in his outbuildings had been started from a spark caused by the explosion at the Sluggish Trout or from an arson attack, particularly as he had not reported it to the Police at the time.

The sheer scale of the Coretec/Fireflow activities and the fact that the rule of law appeared to have been absent while Findlay was injured, meant that the farmers also found it difficult to argue that there had not been a state of Civil Disturbance. It was obvious that the Police had been unable to control the situation or it would not have continued for so long without hindrance. That the farmers themselves had helped create this atmosphere of lawlessness by indulging in a mass brawl that had also led the authorities to think that terrorists were operating in the area, meant that they felt unable to argue too strenuously.

With regard to the stolen and appropriated cattle, the situation for the farming community was even worse. In a typically helpful fashion, the Department for the Environment, Farming and Rural Affairs had sent in its shock troops to investigate the unlicensed movement of livestock and were now proving extremely difficult. Farmers were being forced to complete long and complex forms to try and explain why their beasts had been moved around the countryside without following the rules. Strangely, the investigators seemed to have no interest in the farmers' explanations that the cattle had been stolen. Hungry Knowe, typically, was brusquely told that he had permitted cattle to be moved without a licence. When he pointed out that he had done everything in his power to stop his herd being taken off his land he was then informed that he should have been more careful in adhering to the rules.

Altogether, the farmers had little cause to look favourably on Fang, but Alice, revelling in her new position as lady to the laird, carried out a one-woman charm offensive that had at least ensured that the farmers did not take their animosity to a higher level. When Alice then suggested that the farmers seeks damages from the remnants of Coretec and Fireflow and that she and Fang had waived their right to do so in favour of the farmers, the atmosphere thawed considerably.

Findlay was happily still ensconced in the Police House refusing all offers of promotion or transfer. In between spending inordinate amounts of time in bed with the ever inventive Sonya, he applied himself to being the model rural policeman and was happily writing a textbook on the subject. Far from finding the area or dull and boring, Findlay thoroughly enjoyed himself secure in the knowledge that the majority of the population saw him as their champion in light of the previous summer's events.

Sonya was equally satisfied with life. She did not miss the city at all and she found Findlay suited her ideally. She and Alice met most days at each other's homes and she occasionally did consultancy work, invariably via the Internet that meant she did not have to leave Findlay.

The Church in its broadest sense had enjoyed something of a revival following the defeat of Galphay. The clerics had seized the moment and by dint of hard work were now viewed as miracle workers by other colleagues with less well attended Churches. The Reverend McLeod was happily working hard in Glasgow and endeavouring to write an epic poem in Gaelic. He was aware that he was unlikely to gain a large circulation but it amused him. He was looking forward to next year's summer camp with trepidation, particularly as his student helpers were due to graduate and likely to move away. However, he retained his optimism and that his Lord would provide.

The scouts themselves had followed the newspapers avidly and, in view of his willingness to battle overwhelming odds, allowed the Reverend McLeod to lecture them on their behaviour and encourage them to study unlike everyone else in their lives.

Wear and Sweetness were still living together and amazed mutual acquaintances by seeming happy with each other. They were making a good living on the circuit lecturing on 'Training as an aid not an obsession'. Unlike everyone else, they had drawn different conclusions on the previous summer's events and appeared to believe strongly that it was merely misapplied enthusiasm that had caused the 'difficulties' as they liked to refer to the anarchy that had descended on Bleakhope. They were careful to keep their real thoughts to themselves. In any event, they were busily developing a strong business with a broad customer base.

Detchant Middleton had never forgiven his editor for pulling him off the story before it had broken. Not even in the dead of night could he bring himself to accept that there had been nothing else to do at the time. This feeling of injustice had at least served to spur him on to write a highly coloured book on the depths that the government and its agencies were willing to sink and how any abuse of personal liberties was viewed as acceptable if it reduced a presumed terrorist threat. The book sold inordinately well amongst the intellectual fraternity.

The families of the erstwhile staff of the Sluggish Trout had never discovered what had happened to their missing relatives. All attempts had been met with blank looks and considerable obfuscation. As the authorities were able to hide behind their own legislation regarding the release of information, it was unlikely that they ever would discover the truth.

Mickley, Galphay and their former employees had starred in a major trial that had caused widespread debate and hand wringing. At the end, once the long anticipated guilty verdicts were brought in, the Judge had been savagely condemnatory in his summing up, no one was surprised by the lengths of sentences handed down. The only member of either company to avoid a custodial sentence was the Resources manager whose injuries at the jaws of the police dogs had excited considerable comment in the press and who was seen, even by the Procurator Fiscal as a victim of the criminal conspiracy rather than an active participant. Due to Findlay's prodigious efforts in taking witness statements and ensuring that Coretec and Fireflow were seen as taking over a perfectly valid form of training to satisfy their twisted lust for power, Fang, Alice and, most importantly to him, Sonya were viewed only as witnesses.

Mickley and Galphay were actually quite happy in jail. The fact that the majority of their staff were locked up with them meant that they had an advantage already in gaining position within the prison population. In addition to being seen as vaguely heroic for so blatantly running a district and defying the Police, their ability to call up support from the by now battle hardened ex-employees to handle any disputes, meant that they were now effective twin rulers of the jail.

Bleakhope tower had avoided Fang's plans to renovate it. After studying the building for some time, he had decided to leave well alone. Now, it had settled back into a state of vicious expectation for the old days to return once more.